RUNS WITH COURAGE

Sleeping Bear Press™
2395 South Huron Parkway, Suite 200
Ann Arbor, MI 48104
www.sleepingbearpress.com

Printed and bound in the United States.

10 9 8 7 6 5 4 3 2 1

Library of Congress Cataloging-in-Publication Data
Names: Wolf, Joan M., 1966- author.
Title: Runs with Courage / Joan M. Wolf.
Description: Ann Arbor, MI : Sleeping Bear Press, [2016] |
Summary: In the Dakota Territory in 1880, Four Winds, a ten-year-old
Lakota girl, is taken from her family to a boarding school, where she
is taught English and expected to assimilate into white culture.
Identifiers: LCCN 2016007654 | ISBN 9781585369843 (hard cover)
ISBN 9781585369850 (paper back)
| Subjects: LCSH: Lakota Indians—Juvenile fiction. | CYAC: Lakota
Indians—Fiction. | Indians of North America—Great Plains—Fiction.
| Boarding schools—Fiction. | Schools—Fiction. | Identity—Fiction. | Race
relations—Fiction. | Dakota Territory—Fiction.
Classification: LCC PZ7.W819157 Run 2016 | DDC [Fic]—dc23
LC record available at https://lccn.loc.gov/2016007654

Cover illustration:
Felicia Macheske for Sleeping Bear Press

RUNS WITH COURAGE

BY JOAN M. WOLF

PUBLISHED BY SLEEPING BEAR PRESS

For Jeanie

Let us put our minds together and see what life we will make for our children.

—Tatanka Iyotake (Sitting Bull)

ACKNOWLEDGMENTS

I did not take the writing of this book lightly. It is an important story that is an integral part of our country's history, and one that has difficult truths in it. Besides my own research for this book, I am so grateful to those who helped in the process.

Tremendous thanks to Dr. Ann Robertson, Native American Studies teacher in the Sioux Falls School District and consultant for the Center for American Indian Research and Native Studies, and Jace DeCory, assistant professor in American Indian Studies at Black Hills State University, who both vetted the story for historical and cultural accuracy. Any mistakes are entirely my own.

Many thanks to my editor, Barb McNally, for making the editing process so positive and smooth. And to Catherine Frank, for her editorial insights and thoughts.

Continuing thanks to my agent, Ann Tobias. You are appreciated more than words can express.

Sheila O'Connor, teacher and friend. I thank you for coffee, talks, and encouragement. And to my sister and group of friends who have encircled me with support. You are my everything.

VOCABULARY

Lakota: One of three divisions of the Oceti Sakowin, Seven Council Fires, Native American tribe, living primarily on the western plains of South Dakota

Tiospaye: Lakota term for an extended family group living together in a small community

Tribe: Two or more groups of tiospayes (*tiospaye ki*), whose members collectively form a larger group of Native Americans

He Sapa: Lakota name for the Black Hills

Wasna: A dish that consisted of dried berries, dried buffalo, and fat. Considered a healing dish.

Wotawe: A medicine pouch filled with items that offer protection to its wearer

ONE

BEGINNING

Great Sioux Reservation | Dakota Territory | 1880

The prairie had been very still the day the whites came. The animals stayed tucked in their burrows most of the day. The grasses had not danced in the wind. Clouds had not appeared in the blue sky. It was as if the prairie itself knew of what was to come.

"Sister," Bear said, pointing. "What is that?"

I looked up from the basket I was mending to see a wagon approach in a cloud of dust. I knew immediately it was the whites.

Before Cousin had died from the meat sickness, she and I often talked about them.

"What do you think the whites look like?" she had asked

once as we walked together on the prairie, only a moon before her death.

"They must be very tall. Very powerful," I answered. It was the white's leader, the Great White Father, who had forced us to the Great Sioux Reservation. Only someone very powerful could do that.

"They must look like warriors," Cousin had agreed.

"Yes," I said. "And if we see them, we will be brave like warriors."

Cousin had nodded.

Even though we were girls, we knew we could be as brave as our boy cousins. And like the boys, we too wanted to receive our adult names.

I was in my tenth season and had been called by my childhood name of Four Winds since I could remember. Uncle had given me this name when we still lived in the forest of He Sapa, before our move to the reservation. I had received this name because I could hear the words of our ancestors speaking in the winds that moved through the trees.

Cousin's name had been Laughing Deer because she had long, graceful legs like a deer, and she was always joyful and laughing. Grandfather had given her this name.

I had not talked about the whites with anyone since Cousin had died. But now, they were in front of me.

A white man and woman sat at the front of a large cart pulled by a horse. Their skin was very pale and their clothes were strange. But they were not as tall as I had thought they would be. They looked no more powerful than any of our own warriors.

The woman wore a long black dress that fit tightly at her waist. She had a fabric covering around her head that was tied with a ribbon beneath her chin. The man wore long pants connected to straps on his shirt. The coverings on his feet looked hard and came to a point. They didn't look anything like moccasins. How could he walk in such things?

I couldn't see the color of the woman's hair, but the man's hair was the same golden shade as the prairie grasses. It gleamed in the light of the sun.

"Sister," Bear whispered from my side, "the man's hair. Do you see?" My brother was only five seasons and curious about everything. "It is so short."

Rather than flow down his back, the man's hair stopped at his shoulders as if it had been cut. No one ever cut their hair unless they were mourning.

"I don't know," I whispered. "Perhaps the hair of white men does not grow."

"Sister," he asked, "why are they here?"

I shook my head, unable to answer and unable to stop staring as the two whites and the reservation official who had come with them walked into the council lodge.

I longed for Cousin to be by my side again. She would have ideas about this mysterious appearance in our *tiospaye*. We would talk and giggle until the worry of this unexpected visit would blow away in the breeze. More than anything I wished to hear the sound of her laugh again.

I took Bear by the hand and led him to the other side of our tipi, where we couldn't see what was happening. I began to play a bone game with him, trying to distract both of us from this visit.

But soon one of the aunts came for Bear, and I went to the front of our tipi to watch the council lodge. Whenever someone came in or out, I looked down as if I were stitching a quilled pouch. The aunts and I pretended to work but no one was really working. We were all paying close attention to the lodge.

The whites stayed as the sun crawled halfway down the sky. Elders came into the lodge, left, and came back with other members of our tiospaye. My heart quickened when I saw Uncle emerge from the council lodge and return with Father next to him.

When the aunts gathered to prepare the evening meal, I listened to their chatter. I was not old enough to join their talk, but I could listen.

"Has the Great White Father passed another law?" one of the aunts asked.

"Do you think that's why they have come?" said another.

"Will we have to move again? Are they taking away this land too?"

"Did you see his hair? How can he cut his hair?"

"Their clothes are too tight. And too long. And how do they walk with those hard coverings on their feet?"

I listened to their questions, hoping that when I joined my family for our meal, Father or Uncle would explain why the whites had come.

But that night, the adults were silent. Normally, we would talk as we sat eating together on the floor of the tipi. Father would tell of the day's hunt, and sometimes Uncle would share a story from long ago.

"There were whites here today," I said, unable to keep quiet any longer.

Uncle and Father acted as if they hadn't heard, but Mother put down her buffalo horn spoon and frowned at me.

I knew that as a child it was not my place to be the first to bring up something this important. Mother and the aunts were constantly reminding me how I should be like the other girls, quiet and patient. But quiet was not in my spirit, and my anger was quick to burn.

"You are like lightning, Four Winds," Mother would sometimes scold. "And lightning causes fires."

"Who are the whites?" Bear asked, looking from me to Uncle.

Uncle put down his spoon and looked at Bear thought-fully for several seconds. This was his way. Mother often told me I needed to be more like this, to think carefully before speaking or acting.

"They are men as we are men," Uncle said. "They are two-leggeds who walk upright like us. But inside, they are different." Uncle's voice tightened. "They do not keep their promises. They are not honorable."

"They were here for a long time," I pressed, still wanting to know the reason for their visit. "Are we going to lose this land too?" I asked. Impatience gnawed at me.

Bear looked frightened, and Mother threw an angry glance at me. I shouldn't be scaring my brother with such talk.

No one said anything.

"Will no one talk to me?" I blurted.

"Daughter," Father said quietly. "We will talk when it is time to talk."

I looked down, knowing once again I had acted in a way I should not. *Lightning*, I reminded myself. I had to tame my impatience so it wouldn't burn.

✿ ✿ ✿

For the next moon, I tried to be near my elder relatives as they did their quillwork or tanned hides. I wanted to hear their talk, hoping that some of it would be about the whites and their visit. I was like a rabbit, quiet but aware of everything happening around me.

I thought I could tell when their discussion turned to the topic of the whites. Their voices would fade to a whisper, and they would turn their eyes downward. They always did this when talking of something serious.

I would make my way closer to them, hoping to hear

their discussion. But every time I drew near, their whispers would stop, and they would turn away.

When the moon of cherries blackening appeared, I was happy for something to think about besides the whites. This was the time when the chokecherries ripened and were ready for gathering.

It had been my favorite moon when we had lived in He Sapa. I had loved walking in the forest, finding the bushes of dark tangy berries, picking them by handfuls. I enjoyed helping Mother mash them so they could be mixed into *wasna* to eat during the cold months.

We had not collected any for two seasons because we had been unable to find the berries on the reservation prairie. I had begun to wonder if I would ever taste them again.

"Little Brother," I said on the second day of this moon, "let's look for chokecherries. This is when they are ready to be picked. Do you remember how they make your lips pucker and stain your fingers?"

"A little," he said. He had only been three seasons when we moved to the reservation from the forest. I felt a pang of sadness to know that Bear did not remember much of He Sapa.

I could still remember the sound of the whispering trees

and the feel of the rushing waters. If I closed my eyes, I could even remember the way it smelled of pine.

Mother watched us gather parfleche containers, and I could see in her face that she was skeptical.

"We are going to find chokecherries," I said with determination. "We haven't looked everywhere. There might be bushes growing closer to the rock cliffs."

I took Bear by one hand and picked up a container with the other.

Heat radiated from the ground as we walked through the tall grasses. On the prairie during this moon, the sun acted as a cooking fire, making everything hot and uncomfortable.

But even with the heat, the grasses never seemed to wilt. They grew tall and wild as if they loved the warmth. In some places, they grew taller than Bear.

"Stay close, Little Brother. It is easy to get lost in the grasses," I warned.

"I won't get lost, Sister," he said.

"Uncle gave me the name Four Winds when I was lost once during a chokecherry harvest in He Sapa," I said.

"Were there tall grasses there?" Bear asked.

"No, He Sapa has forests with big trees and cliffs and valleys. It is a sacred place, and it is easy to get lost if you don't pay attention. I was gathering chokecherries with Grandmother and Mother and wandered from them. When Mother found me, I was standing in a clearing of trees above a small ravine. Later, I told Mother I could hear the voices of our ancestors whispering through the wind in the trees. I told her exactly what they had said, even though I was only three seasons."

"Do the tree voices sound like the grass wind?" Bear asked.

"No," I said. "I can't hear voices in the winds here. But sometimes, if I close my eyes, I can still remember the sound of the trees in He Sapa and the words our ancestors spoke in the four winds."

"Are those chokecherries, Sister?" Bear asked, interrupting my story, pointing to a small bush with red berries.

"No, those are poison. Look closely," I said, squishing one of the berries between my fingers. "The color is too red. Chokecherries are much blacker. The birds will eat these, but we will get sick if we do."

He frowned with disappointment but then began running up the bluff we had come to.

"I will find them, Sister! I will find those chokecherries!" he said.

☼ ☼ ☼

But we returned to our tipi late that afternoon to report that we had found none.

Bear had seen a small lizard and he could hardly contain his excitement.

"It has a long tail and walks very close to the earth. It is like a snake but not like a snake," he babbled as we ate watery, thin stew for our evening meal.

None of the adults said anything. It was another meal without speaking. I knew something was wrong.

"We live in the white man's world," Uncle said after Bear had finally stopped talking about the lizard. "This is our reality."

I felt my stomach knot, remembering the visit from the whites the moon before.

"We must know their ways," he continued. "We must learn about them so we can live in this world. Do you understand, Niece?"

I nodded, although I didn't understand what he was saying. I glanced over to see Mother looking down at her hands.

"For this reason you will leave to live with them and attend their school, Four Winds," Uncle finished.

I was so stunned I couldn't think for several seconds.

"What?" I cried, standing. "What do you mean?" Panic

filled me as I suddenly understood why the whites had come. They had come to take me away.

"No!" I said, looking around at my family. "No!"

But my future had been decided. There was nothing to say.

I was outside, running across the prairie before anyone could stop me, as if I could run away from this future. I ran until it felt as if my lungs would explode. Then I collapsed in the tall grasses, trying to catch my breath.

The sun had disappeared and the sky had grown dark. Crickets had begun their night song, and I sat on the ground a long time, letting the sound of their lullaby calm me.

When I returned to our tipi, everyone was still sitting, although the stew had been removed. Bear was playing with stones on top of his sleeping space.

"This is not something you can run from," Uncle said quietly.

I looked down, ashamed that I had let my anger overtake me, ashamed that I had said no to an elder.

"It is a white school for girls only," he continued. "Here you will help us learn the ways of the white world."

Father spoke. "You will learn their language, their customs. And you will teach us. You will help us. Our people need your help."

"This is what has been decided," Uncle finished.
And the discussion ended.

✿ ✿ ✿

That night, Mother came to me as I lay on my sleeping skins.
"Daughter. You are like lightning. You must control your anger before it gets away from you."
"Yes, Mother," I said, feeling tears come to my eyes.
"Be brave," she said, stroking my cheek softly.
Tears were falling now. Mother stayed by my side.
"I will have courage," I said.

✿ ✿ ✿

I fell asleep thinking about Cousin. We had always wanted to prove our bravery, prove that we could be as brave as any warrior.
"We are brave," Cousin had said more than once.
"Yes. We just need the chance to prove it," I agreed.
Now was my chance, the chance I had longed for. I should have felt excited for this moment. But all I felt was fear.

TWO
ARRIVAL

Three suns later, the whites came again in their wagon. This time, I knew why they had come. They had come to take me away.

A different man and woman were in the wagon this time, but they were dressed the same as the other whites. The man wore hard pointed foot coverings, and his hair was cut short. The woman wore a long black dress and a matching headdress that ended in a small piece of ribbon at her chin. They waited near the wagon as I gathered things in our tipi.

Father and Uncle stood outside with Bear, but Mother was inside with me.

"For you," Mother said, placing a small *wotawe* in my hand. It was attached to a leather cord. I looked inside the pouch to see small bits of sage and a tiny piece of buffalo fur.

"To keep you protected," she said. "And to help you remember to use your lightning helpers for strength and not anger."

"Thank you," I said, swallowing back tears.

I slipped the wotawe over my head and stepped outside on legs that felt stiff and hard, like pieces of wood.

"Here, Sister," Bear said, handing me a small carved rabbit. "I made this for you."

Father was teaching Bear to carve. The wooden rabbit was missing an ear and only had one leg. But Bear's eyes shone with pride as he handed it to me.

"It's perfect," I said, squeezing his shoulder. He smiled happily.

I turned to face the wagon.

"Mother," I said softly.

"Courage, Daughter," she said, touching my face with her palm, letting it linger. Father and Uncle both stood tall and I tried to gather courage from their strength. Brother stood between them, bouncing from foot to foot.

The other cousins had left to play, and I was sure he wanted to join them.

Mother held me close, then turned away quickly so I would not see the tears in her eyes.

I was helped into the back of the wagon by the white man.

The white woman began to talk, throwing out words I could not understand. I turned away from her so I could not see the whites but could watch my tipi instead.

With a lurch, the wagon pulled away.

"Sister! Sister!" Bear suddenly cried, trying to break free. But Uncle held his shoulders firmly. I made my face like stone, trying not to show Brother my fear.

I had never ridden in a wagon before, and I found it strange to sit on a large piece of wood that was moving. The wood was vibrating from the wheels' movement, and I could feel my heart beating along fearfully. As the wagon traveled, my tipi shrank to a small speck and finally disappeared completely. I could no longer hold back the tears, and I let them fall down my face.

We rode through the prairie grasses as if the horse were following a path only it could see. The sun had slowly begun to move down the sky, and I watched the grasses sway in the wind as the light dimmed.

The woman had stopped trying to talk to me long before, and I turned to the front of the wagon. I listened to the man and woman talk back and forth with their white words. The words were short, as if a bird's wings had been clipped and it could no longer fly properly. They did not flow one into the other as our words did.

In the fading light, I could barely see the outlines of the bluffs in the distance that were near my tiospaye. Instinctively, I looked up to find the polestar. It had appeared in the sky, a shining light of familiarity, and I watched it as we traveled.

Uncle had told me stories of this star. It was the only star that stayed in one place in the night sky, and it could help someone find their way if they were lost.

Darkness continued to deepen, and I could no longer see shapes in the land. Other stars had begun to appear, twinkling from high above. In the distance, I could see tiny specks of light that looked like stars, but I knew they were not. They were too close to the ground and did not flicker as real stars did.

For a moment, my fear was replaced by curiosity as I studied the lights. They grew larger as we traveled, and eventually I could see they were neither in the sky nor on the ground but were coming from several structures. I realized this was where the wagon was destined, and fear knotted my stomach again.

Finally we stopped in front of one of the structures. It was unlike any tipi I had ever seen, at least three times as high and shaped like a box. We had arrived at the school.

The man and woman climbed down from the wagon and motioned to me to follow.

"No, no!" I cried, trembling. What was left of my courage fled, and I gripped the sides of the wagon tightly. The man and woman just stood watching me.

An opening appeared in the structure, and a different white woman emerged. She too had pale skin and wore a long black dress but she had no headdress. She spoke to the other two and then came to me. Gently, she put one hand over mine, speaking quiet words I couldn't understand. Even though they were the chopped words of the whites, they were words of softness and reminded me of the way Aunt used to comfort me when I was frightened. The woman smiled, and I allowed her to pull my hand away from the side and help me out of the wagon.

I followed her through the opening in the tall structure. Once inside I stopped, unable to keep walking. The space was open like a tipi, but it looked as if it were made of wood instead of buffalo skins. There were no sleeping skins or cooking fires, nothing to show that anyone lived there. It wasn't rounded and soft like a tipi but hard and rough in places. Above me was wood, and when I looked up, I couldn't see a flap at the top for a cooking fire, just a long flat surface.

The woman tugged my hand to follow, but I was frozen by fear. I shook my head no. She ignored this and pulled me toward a smaller narrow space where there were long pieces of wood stacked on top of one another. It looked as if they went up into the wall. Dropping my hand, the woman began to climb the wooden pieces, then turned and motioned for me to follow as she disappeared beyond the wall.

I was sure this was some sort of white man's magic, and I stopped for a moment. But I was terrified of being left alone, so I hurried to follow her. As I climbed to the top, I discovered a long space. The woman walked through this space and into a room.

I peeked in to see a room of sleeping spaces in two neat rows. Each sleeping space stood above the floor on small wooden sticks that kept it propped high. There were no skins rolled out on the floor. Did the whites sleep up off the ground?

The woman led me to one that had clothing laid across it and showed me that she wanted me to dress in this clothing.

I picked up something that looked like a white dress and rubbed it between my fingers. It felt rough and coarse, nothing like the clothing Mother had sewn from deer hide. This dress looked too long and too large. I shook my head no.

The woman frowned, murmuring white words, then abruptly turned and left me standing in the room alone.

I continued to stand there, unsure of what to do next. For the first time in my life, I was away from my tiospaye, away from everyone I knew, everyone who cared about me. I looked around for anything familiar, but everything I saw felt wrong. The sleeping spaces were up off the ground and covered with blankets instead of skins. The walls were made of wood instead of buffalo hide. The floor was made of wood instead of earth, and I knew that I was standing on a place that was stacked on top of another place. I had never been in a tipi that had one open space stacked upon another.

On a wall I could see a picture of a man hanging from two pieces of crossed wood. His hands had been pierced and attached to the wood, and his face was filled with agony. Clearly, he had been injured. Was this meant as a warning to me?

Suddenly exhausted, I slid to the floor, not trusting that I would be safe sitting on the sleeping space when it was so high above the ground.

I heard footsteps and voices, and I stood as girls walked into the room. Each wore a dress similar to the woman's, except the dresses were blue and pink and yellow instead of black. Each girl had neatly trimmed hair, and they were all speaking in the strange clipped words of the whites. At first, I thought they were white girls.

But their skin was the same color as mine, and I realized they were Lakota, like me.

The girls stared at me as they walked by, and I stood in the middle of the room, staring back at them. A different white woman had come in behind them and she stood smiling at me. But I remained in my place, still unsure of what I was supposed to do.

Finally one of the girls came to me and led me to a sleeping space, whispering quietly in Lakota.

"It is nighttime. We say prayers and sleep. Watch and do the same."

The white woman cleared her throat, and all the girls went to a sleeping space and knelt beside it, pressing their hands together.

"Do the same," repeated the girl, pulling me down to my knees.

The woman spoke words, and the girls spoke the same words.

Then everyone changed into the same kind of dress that had been laid out for me. I realized the clothing on my sleeping space was meant to be nightclothes.

But why couldn't I sleep in the clothes I had brought with me, clothes that were comfortable and familiar? I threw the ugly white dress off my sleeping space and lay down on top, feeling dizzy with anger and confusion.

The woman came to me and frowned, picking the nightdress up from the floor, folding it neatly, and placing it at the bottom of my sleeping space. Then she sat next to me and stroked my forehead. I closed my eyes and swallowed hard. Her touch was kind and gentle, and I could feel myself close to tears. But I would not show weakness by crying. I bit the inside of my cheek and turned away from her until she stood and left. After she was gone, I kicked the dress off the sleeping space once again.

Someone blew out the lanterns, and the room fell into darkness. I lay on top of my sleeping space, still in the clothing in which I had come, staring through a small space in the wall where I could see outside. A few lonely stars stared back through the blackness.

"My name is Walks Tall," I heard a whisper from the sleeping space next to mine. "It will get easier," she said.

I traced the outline of the small rabbit Bear had carved for me. Loneliness pushed down on me like a heavy blanket, and I finally let the tears come.

Where's your courage now? I could imagine Cousin saying.

I desperately wished she was next to me, still alive.

"Here it is, Cousin, right here," I whispered, trying to stop the tears, trying to find courage that I was afraid had disappeared forever.

THREE
BRAVE

Loud clanging startled me awake, and I opened my eyes to sun streaming into the room. At first, I couldn't remember where I was. But then the sounds of other girls brought the memory rushing back.

"You must dress." I heard hushed Lakota and looked up to see the girl who called herself Walks Tall peering at me. Her hair was loose from its braids, and I could see that it ended beneath her shoulders in a neat, straight line. I shuddered. It had been cut.

I took a step back and shook my head no.

"You must," she whispered. "It is the rule here."

She went to the small trunk by my sleeping space and

pulled out a dress.

"But they are not my clothes," I said loudly, angrily.

All movement in the room stopped, every pair of eyes turning to me.

Another girl leaned close to my face. "Never speak Lakota out loud," she whispered fiercely. "Never. It is against the rules."

I clutched the front of the dress Mother had made me. It was soft and held the scent of prairie. I pulled it over my head and laid it across my bed, then stepped into the dress that had been left for me. It felt coarse and scratchy against my skin. It was unlike anything I had ever worn before, and I wondered what kind of animal it had come from. It was pink in color, dotted with small flowers that didn't look anything like real flowers.

"That is not allowed," Walks Tall whispered, pointing to my wotawe, which was still around my neck.

"But . . . ," I said, grasping it in my hand.

"They will take it if they see it," she continued.

Carefully, I pulled the small pouch over my head and tucked it inside my own deerskin dress, next to the small wooden rabbit, for safekeeping. I did not want the whites to take these things from me.

The other girls sat and began to put on foot coverings. I searched beneath my sleeping space and found my own pair. I pulled one out and studied it. It was black and hard with small strings running along one side. I looked down at the moccasins I was still wearing. They formed to my feet perfectly.

I watched the other girls pull the strings in and through small clasps on either side of their foot coverings. I slipped off my moccasins and picked up one of the coverings, forcing my foot down into its hard rigid shape. Instantly my toes cried out in pain. I tried to wiggle them but couldn't. When I stood, I couldn't even walk. I pulled the foot covering off and tossed it beneath the sleeping space, angry again that I could not wear my own clothes. I would wear the dress, but for this day I would go without anything on my feet.

The girls began leaving the room, and I followed them all the way down the strange stacked pieces of wood and into the large open space. I looked up and realized the sleeping place was above us. I shuddered. How could one place stay above another without crashing down?

The girls continued through the large space and into a smaller room where there were two large thin pieces of wood. Each was held up off the ground by wooden legs. Every girl went to one and pulled something away, sitting down on it. It did not appear that they were going to sit on the ground and eat. It looked as if we were meant to eat off the long pieces of wood.

One of the women came to me and smiled, pointing to show that I should sit at one of the long pieces of wood.

"Table," she said.

I hesitated. I had never seen something so high off the ground that I was supposed to sit on. Two girls from the night before beckoned me toward them, and I carefully lowered myself to sit. They each smiled briefly, then turned back and whispered to each other.

"They are sisters," Walks Tall whispered in Lakota. "They talk more to each other than to anyone else." I nodded, looking at them again and realizing that they did look like sisters.

The woman who had brought me into the school the night before came to me and pulled my leg away from the table, pointing to my bare foot. Angrily, I yanked my leg back, but she grabbed it again and spoke in loud white words. Another woman came over and shook her head, saying words back. Then both turned away.

"You are lucky," Walks Tall whispered to me in Lakota. "Miss Beatrice told Miss Agnes that she thinks it is okay for you to go without shoes today."

"Is that what the foot coverings are called?" I asked.

She nodded, and I nodded back. But I did not feel lucky.

I realized the other girls were staring at me, and I shoved my feet beneath the table, feeling my cheeks grow warm from anger and embarrassment.

Then all of the girls grew quiet, folded their hands, and looked down. One of the women began to speak, and the girls joined her, murmuring the same words she was speaking.

I had never heard speaking where everyone said the same words at the same time. Most of my tiospaye's songs were made up as needed, to tell what was happening or what had happened. I loved our songs, our dances.

I looked around at the other girls and felt a sharp pinch on my ear. The woman who had grabbed my foot towered over me, glaring, her fingers ready to pinch again. I quickly pressed my hands together and looked down like everyone else.

The speaking finished, and the girls began to eat. I touched the small round object sitting in front of me and watched, fascinated, as the girls took food from large bowls and put it on their own round circles. I realized they were circles to eat from.

I rubbed mine, feeling how smooth it was. It did not feel like anything I had touched before. When I tapped it with my finger, I heard a soft clinking sound. I picked it up to discover it was light and smooth on the bottom too. Two long silver pieces of metal lay on each side of my eating circle.

I watched to see what the other girls were doing. They were using the metal pieces to put food into their mouths. The pieces looked a little like the spoons I was used to. I picked one up but found I couldn't make it do what I wanted it to. It was too thin, too long. In frustration, I set it down on the table and crossed my arms. I didn't need to eat.

"Here," Walks Tall whispered in Lakota, handing me a small piece of food. "This is bread. Eat this. It's easier."

"Thank you," I mumbled, grateful for the help.

The bread was warm in my hand. It looked like nothing I had eaten before. I sniffed it and tore a small piece away. The outer cover was crunchy, but it was soft inside.

"Miss Beatrice made it today," Walks Tall said, watching me. "It's one of her special recipes. Try it. It's delicious."

I took a small bite and discovered it tasted a little sweet. It tasted so good I hungrily gobbled the entire piece.

I put my hands in my lap, waiting quietly.

"You can eat more," Walks Tall whispered, pointing to a bowl that was still filled with pieces of bread.

"Are you sure?" I whispered back. I couldn't believe this was possible.

She nodded. "There is no hunger here."

I had never been able to eat so much. I had always finished a meal almost as hungry as when I had started.

I took bite after bite, almost afraid if I stopped eating, the food would disappear. But as soon as one bowl of bread was empty, more bread would appear. It was as if the food was growing from the bowl itself. How I wished Bear could be here and eat as much as he wanted.

When the other girls started to leave, I followed, but felt my stomach clench in pain from all the bread I had eaten. I sat back down, doubling over, trying not to throw up.

The woman who had pinched my ear took my arm and led me back up to our sleeping room. She pointed to my sleeping space, and I sat. Then she turned and left.

If I were with my tiospaye, one of my aunts would have given me a piece of medicine bark to chew on. An aunt would have sat with me and helped soothe my stomach.

Instead, I sat alone on my strange high-up sleeping space, trying to ignore the pain.

Suddenly I smelled smoke and jumped up, panicked, trying to find what was burning. I could see nothing inside that was on fire, so I went to the small clear place in the wall that you could look through. Outside, on the ground below, a boy with short hair was throwing clothes into the flames of a small fire.

"No!" I said when I realized he had the deerskin dress Mother had made for me.

I ran back to my sleeping space and tore the blanket and pillow away, hoping to find my clothes where I had left them. But there was nothing there.

Back at the clear space, I looked down to see the ends of my dress being consumed by the flames, Mother's wotawe and Bear's rabbit along with it.

"No! Stop!" I yelled, and realized the white boy couldn't hear me. "No!" I pounded my fists against the clear space.

The boy looked up briefly, and I jumped back. He was not white. His skin color and eyes were the same as mine. He was Lakota. But his hair was short, like that of the white man.

I lay back on my sleeping space. The white food had become a hard lump in my stomach, and I tried to ignore the nausea. The only things I had from home had been reduced to ash. I curled into a ball and cried myself to sleep.

✧ ✧ ✧

When I awoke, my stomach felt better. The sun had traveled far down in the sky, and the light outside was fading. I went to the clear space to see if the boy was still there, but all I could see in the dim light was a pile of burned logs.

There was a rustle behind me, and I jumped. The woman who had made the bread was standing in the doorway. Miss Beatrice.

She struck a match and lit the oil lamps, then walked over to my sleeping space and sat down, touching a place next to her. I approached cautiously and stood near her. She patted the place again, and I sat.

Words came from her mouth, and even though I couldn't understand them, I could tell they were words of kindness. From within her long black dress, she pulled out a small piece of bread and offered it to me. Just seeing the bread made my stomach turn, and I shook my head forcefully.

The other girls came in, and the woman greeted them,

talking in white words. The girls answered, also using white words.

They each crawled into their sleeping spaces, and the woman walked around, touching the girls' heads and speaking softly to them.

Her hand lingered when she came to me, and she patted my shoulder. Then she blew out the lamps one by one, and the room fell into darkness.

"She is one of the nice ones," Walks Tall whispered. "She doesn't hit us." She was speaking in Lakota.

"You get hit here?" I whispered back, horrified.

"Sometimes," someone else answered from my other side. In the dark it was just voices detached from bodies.

"If we talk in Lakota. Or break a rule," Walks Tall answered.

"Why would Uncle and Father send me to such a place?" I asked.

No one answered.

In the dim outline of the moon I could just make out the man hanging on the wall, broken and bleeding, reminding me to follow the rules.

FOUR
SCHOOL

The next day I felt stronger, determined to be brave. I had been sent here for a reason. I could not doubt the wisdom of Uncle and the other elders. I would learn all I could about the white world at this school so that I could help my people understand these new ways.

"They call me Four Winds," I said quietly to Walks Tall as we dressed.

She nodded but said, "You are not allowed to use that name in front of the teachers. We are not allowed to use our names here."

"Why? What's wrong with my name?"

"They say it is a heathen name," another girl answered,

a girl I would learn was called Moon Awake by her tiospaye.

"But what is a heathen?" I asked.

"Someone who is not Christian," Walks Tall answered.

"But what is a Christian?" I asked, feeling even more confused.

"Someone who worships the white god," Moon Awake answered.

"But who is the white god? Is he here? Is he the same as the Great White Father?" I persisted.

"You ask too many questions," Moon Awake said. "You will learn all of this in church services."

I had no idea what church services were and wanted to ask. But I knew I had already asked too many questions. I would have to be patient and find out on my own.

At morning meal, I paid close attention to the chanting of the girls, trying to remember some of the clipped white words from the day before. I ate little bits of bread instead of whole mouthfuls, and I stopped eating after a few pieces.

When the meal was finished, the girls stood and picked up their eating circles.

"Now we bring our dishes to the pantry," Walks Tall whispered.

"Is that what this is called?" I whispered back, pointing to my eating circle.

"That is called a plate. Plates are also called dishes."

I nodded as if I understood.

"We take turns washing dishes," Walks Tall continued. "Today is not my turn, and it is time to go to lessons. Follow me."

I turned to follow. But the woman who had pinched my ear the day before stopped me and said white words to Walks Tall. Walks Tall took my plate and went to the pantry. The woman took my arm and led me to another room, where someone else stood holding something I had never seen before. It looked like two small knives that were somehow attached.

I drew away, realizing there were no other girls in the room. Before I knew what was happening, the woman holding the two knives tool grabbed my shoulders, turned me around, and took my hair. I heard a snipping sound.

"No, no, stop!" I cried, begging in Lakota, realizing she was cutting my hair. I strained against her hands, grabbing at my hair, trying to protect it. I was not in mourning. My hair should not be cut.

The woman only yanked harder, refusing to let go,

continuing to snip. I could feel sharp stings on my neck as I struggled.

She stopped momentarily, and I tried to escape, running toward the opening in the wall space. But the woman grabbed my arm, twisting it painfully, and slapped me hard against the cheek.

She took my chin in one hand and tilted my face so that it was close to hers.

"No!" she said.

It was the first white word I learned.

I stood still, watching pieces of myself fall to the ground like dead insects. I could feel my hair being put into braids, and I thought of the times Aunt would comb it, telling me stories as she did so. I loved the feel of her fingers running through my hair and the sound of her voice rising and falling in story.

"We do not cut our hair unless we are in mourning," Aunt would remind me as she sat combing and braiding my hair. I could still remember the crackle of the fire and the way it danced in the darkness when she sat with me.

"I won't cut my hair, Aunt," I had promised when I was six seasons. "Never."

This time of hair braiding had been a time of connection

between the two of us. But this felt like a punishment.

Someone else led me back through the eating space and outside toward a large structure that was also made of wooden walls. As we walked, I traced the new short row of hair that now rested on my forehead. I touched the little cuts on my neck that had been made as I had struggled. I looked down to see my fingertips dotted with blood.

The door to the structure opened, and I could see the kind woman, the one named Miss Beatrice, standing and talking in front of a large room. Did she know they had just cut my hair? Did she understand what this meant?

All of the other girls were inside this room too, sitting in rows, each at their own table.

Miss Beatrice stopped talking, and the girls turned and watched me walk in.

I was led to my own place and pushed to sit down next to Walks Tall. Miss Beatrice began speaking again in her white words, and all of the girls turned their attention back to her. I took hold of one of my braids, feeling hot, angry tears on my cheeks.

"I know," Walks Tall whispered in Lakota. "I understand."

I looked away from her, not wanting to talk to anyone.

In front of me was a small piece of thin stone that I had

seen before in He Sapa. Walks Tall nudged me and picked up hers, showing me how to hold it.

"Slate board," Walks Tall said, pointing to her stone, using a white word that sounded strange to my ears.

"Pencil," she added, showing me how she made marks on her slate board with her pencil. Even though the pencil was black, it made white marks.

As Miss Beatrice continued to talk, I studied the other girls. They were sitting quietly and watching the white woman. No one spoke. No one stood or moved around. Everyone sat and listened, making marks on their slates with the things called pencils.

I continued to look around the room and gasped when I saw someone sitting alone toward the back. It was the boy who had burned my clothes, the boy who had cut his hair to be as short as the white man's.

"Who is that?" I whispered, grabbing Walks Tall's arm.

She looked alarmed at the fear in my voice but then saw where I was looking.

"Oh, that's just the boy William," she said reassuringly.

"I thought this was a school for girls," I said.

"It is. But William is different. He is slow. He gathers wood and fixes things and helps with chores. They let him listen to lessons, but he's just here to help the teachers. I don't think he can learn. They let him stay because they feel sorry for him."

"He burned my clothes," I said, feeling a lump in my throat. "I hate him."

She nodded. "You should stay away from him. He is slow."

✵ ✵ ✵

A metal bell clanged and I jumped. All at once, the girls stood and began to sing, and I felt my spirit soar. Singing. Dancing. Finally I could dance my dance of grief, of cutting hair, of confusion and uncertainty. I so loved the dance and the singing and the way you could share joy and sadness through both.

I stood, ready to begin the dance, but the singing was wrong. And there was no dancing. Each girl had her hands pressed together, and everyone was singing the same words at the same time, voices rising and falling in similar pitch and tone. It sounded like a song of death.

When the singing finished, the girls walked outside, talking to one another. I followed, unsure of where they were going or what was happening next.

"The bell tells us that it is now time to eat," Walks Tall whispered as Moon Awake took my arm and led me to a large tree.

I could hear birds singing above, and I looked up, comforted by the familiar sound. Perhaps one would carry the message back to my tiospaye that I was lonely, that the whites had cut my hair even though I had not wanted them to.

Moon Awake pointed to a spot on the ground near a large tree, and the three of us sat. Walks Tall passed a small metal bucket around that had bits of bread and dried meat inside.

But instead of eating, I pulled at my newly trimmed hair.

"They cut my hair," I said softly in Lakota.

Both girls continued eating, neither one speaking.

"And yours." I reached over and touched one of Moon Awake's braids.

Walks Tall shrugged.

"They cut my hair," I said loudly, not caring if anyone heard me speak Lakota. "They cut your hair too! How can you not care about this?" I was practically screaming now.

There was a slap, and I felt my ear stinging. I looked up

into the face of the woman who had pinched my ear the day before. A stream of angry white words flowed from her mouth. The nice woman, Miss Beatrice, came and began talking with the woman who had slapped me.

Gradually the first woman's face grew less angry. She pinched my ear one last time, then turned and walked away. Miss Beatrice came to me, and I flinched. But she put her hand on my shoulder and made a talking motion with her hands against her mouth.

"No," she said forcefully. Then she turned and followed the other woman.

"I told you not to speak in Lakota," Walks Tall whispered.

"It is not allowed," Moon Awake added.

I lost the battle against my anger, and I was up and running, escaping blindly across the prairie in shoes that didn't fit right, in a dress that was confining and tight. Who were these people to take me from my tiospaye and cut my hair?

I could hear white words behind me, calling, calling. But I was running like the wind, fast and strong and invisible, until suddenly there were arms wrapped around me and I was on the ground in a tangle with Walks Tall.

"You must return," she said softly in Lakota.

I looked up to see Miss Beatrice approaching, breathing

heavily, followed by several other girls.

"It will get easier," Walks Tall whispered.

The anger left suddenly, like a puff of smoke released from a fire, and I was filled with sadness. Tears began falling, and I could not stop them. Moon Awake and Walks Tall sat next to me and patted my legs until slowly the tears stopped. No one said anything, and I sat without moving until Walks Tall helped me up, and the three of us walked back.

"Sarah. Sarah," Miss Beatrice kept repeating. And that was when I learned my second white word, my new name, Sarah.

"But what is a Sarah?" I asked that night as everyone lay in our sleeping spaces. "What does it mean? How did I earn this name?"

"You don't earn names here. They are just given," Moon Awake answered.

"But, Walks Tall," I persisted, "why can't I use my name? Why can't I be called Four Winds?"

"Because that is your Lakota name," she said. "You will be hit if you use it. My white name is Anna. You must call me this name when we are with the whites. Moon Awake is known as Ella."

"But those names mean nothing," I said. "How will I know who is brave or who has knowledge of medicine or who can help with cooking?"

Walks Tall shrugged.

Sarah. I rolled the name around in my head, trying to get used to its emptiness. It described nothing about me.

"My name is Four Winds," I persisted. "Uncle gave me this name because I can understand the speaking of winds in the trees. I am not this 'Sarah' they keep calling me. What is a Sarah? I don't know."

No one answered.

"Well, I can give names too," I said. "The one who pinches my ear and who slapped me—"

"That is Miss Agnes," someone interrupted.

"Not anymore," I snapped. "She is called Pinch Finger."

Someone giggled.

"And why are there only women here?" I continued. "Why are there no brothers or fathers? And where are the cousins, the children of the women?"

"The whites do not teach their children in the same places where they live. It is not like a tiospaye. The whites live in houses and teach their children in places called schools," Walks Tall explained.

"The women are the teachers here, but there is one man who visits. He is the pastor. His name is Pastor Huber," Moon Awake added.

"And there is the boy William," Walks Tall said. "He does chores and fixes things that break."

"Where is his tiospaye?" I asked. "Why do they not want him? What's wrong with him?"

Moon Awake shrugged. "No one knows. He doesn't talk. He's slow."

It was all too confusing, and I turned away and stopped talking. Eventually, the other girls stopped talking too, and I could tell they had fallen asleep.

I crept out of my sleeping space as quietly as I could and made my way to the clear place in the wall where I could see the stars. I searched for the polestar but couldn't find it. If I were outside, I could find it. I could follow it home. I could leave this place and run back to my tiospaye.

I sat thinking for a long while. The elders had sent me to this place, and I trusted their wisdom. I could not disobey them by running away.

But did they really know what happened at the school? Did they know it was a place where children were hit and hair was cut?

I wrestled with these two questions until finally I crawled back into my sleeping space.

I closed my eyes, wishing for the sounds of my family around me. But all I could hear were the sounds of strangers.

I had never felt so alone.

FIVE
LEARNING

For the next moon I felt like a rabbit that had been plucked from its home on the prairie, dropped in a pond, and expected to swim like a duck.

As hard as I tried, I could not seem to go through a lesson or an activity without breaking a rule I didn't even know existed.

"No, Sarah! That is not correct!" I would hear from the teacher named Miss Margaret.

"Sarah, that is not how we do things!" Miss Beatrice would say.

Crack!

I would feel the sting of a ruler coming down on my

knuckles because I had said or done something wrong or spoken out loud in Lakota.

Lightning, I could hear Mother saying when I felt my anger flare and I wanted to scream or run or hit back. *Do not be like the lightning.*

I tried, but sometimes my anger flashed and struck before I could stop it.

One day toward the end of my first moon at the school, I grabbed the ruler away from the teacher I called Pinch Finger before she could hit me with it.

"Enough!" I screamed in Lakota, throwing the ruler to the ground. "Enough!" And I stormed out of the schoolhouse.

I made my way back to my sleeping space and gathered the few clothes that I had. They were white clothes, but they would have to do.

I started across the yard and saw the boy William. I silently dared him to stop me. I wanted a fight so I could let my anger out.

He stood looking at me, and I stared defiantly back.

"I'm leaving, and there is nothing you can do," I spat at him. He continued staring but did nothing to stop me.

I made it all the way across the field near the school

before I was stopped. Miss Margaret appeared, almost as if from nowhere, and grabbed my shoulder.

"What are you doing, Sarah?" she asked, yanking at my arm.

I didn't answer.

"I asked you; what are you doing?" she repeated, her eyes flashing angrily.

Something about her question made the anger inside go away. What was I doing?

I couldn't just run away. I could not bring dishonor to my family. Once again I had reacted without thinking.

I no longer resisted as Miss Margaret dragged me across the yard toward the school.

"My goodness, Sarah. It is dangerous out there. And your parents want you to be here. Why would you waste such an opportunity?" she muttered, more to herself than to me.

The boy had appeared again, standing in his usual way. I turned away so I wouldn't have to see him.

Miss Margaret took my clothes and pushed me into the schoolroom. Pinch Finger looked up briefly, then back down again. For the rest of the afternoon she made me stand at the back of the classroom, holding books in each arm. Their weight grew and grew, and by the time she took the books back, my arms were numb.

"Usually you get hit if you try to run," Moon Awake said as she walked past me while I tried to shake feeling back into my arms.

Walks Tall nodded.

✻ ✻ ✻

I knew my behavior was different from the other girls. I knew it was improper to defy an adult. But in my tiospaye, no adult hit a child. Not ever. I could not understand this form of punishment.

And I could not understand the way of learning at the school. As a child, I had learned about many things by listening to the elders' stories in the camp circle. I learned when Uncle talked with my family about how the stars were connected in the sky and how White Buffalo Calf Woman had first brought her gift to our people. Mother had taught me about plants and berries and how the bark from a willow tree could stop a fever and the coneflower could help with insect bites. I had learned to quill and bead and cook by watching her and my aunts.

But the learning at the school was so different. Every day we would gather in the schoolroom and sit at the hard wooden things called desks. The teacher was the only one who spoke, and she would speak at us about different things. If a girl wanted to talk, she had to stand first and wait for the teacher to come to her or call out her name.

I would often grow tired of listening to the teacher and I would find myself looking around the room. Sometimes I would study the other girls, who always seemed to understand the words the teacher spoke. Other times I would watch the boy, the way he slouched when sitting and stumbled when walking. Mostly, everyone ignored him, but even he was hit sometimes.

Besides hitting, the teachers punished in other ways, I learned. I discovered that words can hurt your spirit like the ruler can hurt your knuckles.

During a manuscript lesson one day, I worked hard to make my letters match the handwriting example Miss Margaret had written on the board. I was still trying to get used to making short marks fit together in the things called words. In my tiospaye there had been no words, no writing. Before coming to the white school, I had only seen pictures used to tell stories.

I finished writing the sentence, then stood and waited for Miss Margaret to check my work.

"Beautiful," she said, smiling.

I was filled with such joy that I began to dance, letting my happiness flow out so others could see.

But instead of joining me in celebration, the room grew silent. The girls huddled over their slates, suddenly working very intently. No one looked at me.

I stopped, knowing I had done something wrong but unsure what it was.

"That is the behavior of a savage," Miss Margaret said loudly. Her face had lost its smile.

I looked down, ashamed. I didn't know what the word *savage* meant, but I knew it wasn't a good word.

"We do not dance like savages," Miss Margaret continued. "When we are happy, we smile and nod. We do not dance this . . . dance. We are civilized, educated. Do you understand, Sarah?"

I nodded, not looking up.

"Then continue with your lesson," she said, turning and walking back to the front of the room.

✿ ✿ ✿

"But I don't understand," I would whisper to Moon Awake or Walks Tall at night after the oil lamps had been put out.

This was when we spoke in Lakota, sharing stories from our elders and repeating stories we had heard as children.

"What is the word *savage*?" I asked.

"It means bad," Walks Tall answered quietly.

"Dirty," Moon Awake added.

"Is this what they think of us? That we're bad? That we're dirty?" I asked, shocked.

"Not always," one of the sisters said. "I think they like us mostly."

"What do you mean, mostly?" I asked, feeling angry and hurt.

"Well, they just don't like it when we act uncivilized."

I exploded.

"Uncivilized?" I cried, getting out of bed and standing. "What is civilized about hitting people? Is that civilized? I don't understand how you let them hit you, how you let them cut your hair. I don't understand how you repeat the prayer words over and over that sound dead and mean-ingless. How can you stand any of it?"

Moon Awake was suddenly standing in front of me, her face close to mine, her hands balled into fists at her sides.

"You have so many questions all of the time," she said through clenched teeth. "Here is a question for you."

I waited, feeling just as angry as she looked.

"Since coming to this school, have you been hungry?" she asked.

"No," I said.

I thought of Bear going to sleep hungry many nights. I thought of how thin my mother was. On the reservation I had always felt hunger. But at the school I had never had so much food. I had never been hungry.

"Before I came here, half of my tiospaye died from hunger," Moon Awake continued, with a catch in her voice. "Sometimes, we went days without food in our bellies. But at this place, no one is dying. No one is hungry."

I nodded.

"So that is why I say their silly prayer songs and speak in their white words and let them cut my hair," she finished.

"Food," I murmured, thinking about how empty my belly had felt on the reservation and how full it felt at the school. Suddenly I could see Bear's face and wished he could join me. Suddenly I was sad instead of angry.

"That is why we surrendered to the reservation when the Great Father ordered it," Moon Awake said quietly.

"That is the only reason. My tiospaye could not hunt because there was no game on the reservation lands, and we weren't allowed to leave the lands. And the food rations were not enough. We were starving."

I nodded. Food was what had brought our surrender too.

"But their food rations caused more death," I said. "The reservation officials promised us cattle, and the scouts thought they would hunt again. But the cattle were delivered already dead and filled with meat sickness. After we ate some, the meat sickness spread through our camp quickly. My brother almost died. And Cousin"—I swallowed hard—"she died from the sickness."

"They promised food. But they broke that promise," Walks Tall said plainly.

"Grandfather says the Great White Father breaks all his promises," one of the younger girls named Small Rose added.

I nodded. I had come to hate the Great White Father.

All around me I heard the sounds of sympathy. Our stories were different but the same. Each of us knew death well. It had lived among our people like a trickster spirit, stealing from us those we loved the most.

SIX
BRIDGE

Over the next two moons I learned to hide my anger, to let it simmer beneath the surface without erupting. I began to understand the teachers and their ways. I recognized some of the words being used in their prayers. And I began to understand what was being taught during lessons.

"Look at this!" I said, poking Moon Awake the first time I recognized that the little stick marks on a page were coming together to form the white word for dog. "I know it! It is the word *dog*!" I practically screamed.

She rolled her eyes at me. "*Dog*. Such a small word. I can read much bigger words than that."

But I didn't care. I was proud of myself.

All around me I began to notice that the same sticks and words were on other things in the white world; on maps, pictures, and papers. As my understanding unfolded, I felt like the prairie awakening in the spring. I was hit with the ruler less. My name was called out in anger less. And I began to feel more settled.

At night, I would look up at the picture of the man on the wall in our sleeping room and feel less afraid that I would be punished as he was.

It was in the church service that I learned more about this man on the wall, the man the whites called Jesus. On the day called Sunday, we didn't have school lessons. Instead, we went into the church building for a church service. The only man I ever saw at the school, Pastor Huber, would be waiting there.

He was always dressed in black, and his hair was cut as short as the boy William's. The teachers called him brother, but he was not a real brother to any of them.

"God is in everything," he would say during church service, pounding his fist on his wooden stand with each word. "He is in all things. Above all else, this you must understand! He will punish the sinners and the nonbelievers."

The first time I heard talk of this god and his punishment, I looked around, frightened. Where was this white god? How could he be everywhere? And how would he punish me?

None of the other girls seemed afraid. So I tried not to be afraid too. I tried to listen and understand.

At the lesson after the church service, Pinch Finger would speak more of the white god.

"God loves you," she said, her voice strong and sure.

"But if this god loves us, why does he punish us too?" I whispered to Moon Awake. "Pastor Huber said that he punishes sinners."

Moon Awake shrugged. "You ask too many questions," she said.

"Ella, if you believe in God fully and live your life for Him, what happens when you die?" Pinch Finger asked.

"You go to heaven," Moon Awake answered.

"Yes!" the teacher said. "And, Ruth, what is in heaven?"

"Food," Small Rose answered, a dreamy look in her eyes.

"Well, yes, I suppose you are correct," Pinch Finger said, sighing. "But after you die you will no longer need food. Do you understand?"

Small Rose nodded agreeably, but I knew she didn't understand. I didn't understand either, and I was frustrated that no one could answer my questions about the white god.

"Jesus died for your sins," Pinch Finger continued, pointing to a picture of the man hanging on the crossed pieces of wood.

I wiggled with impatience. I couldn't sit still when I didn't understand. Finally I stood timidly and waited to be called on.

"Sarah?" Pinch Finger called my name hesitantly. I had never stood to ask a question before.

"Who hurt *this* Jesus?" I asked in my halting white words.

"It's not this Jesus. It's just Jesus. And it was the sinners who hurt him," she answered. "But it was all part of God's plan," she finished quickly.

I sat down, more confused than before I had asked the question.

After the lesson, we filed out of the church, ready for the hour of reflection. This was a time when we were expected to read the book called the Bible.

The air felt crisp and cool, and I looked up and realized the trees were bare. When had I stopped noticing the changing of the season? In my tiospaye, the seasons decided our activities and movements. But at the school, all I paid attention to were the sounds of metal bells clanging and the movement of the white clocks.

I shook my head, trying not to think of this and went to our sleeping space for my hour of reflection. Because I wasn't able to read the Bible yet, I had other books I would read instead.

Miss Beatrice had given me the third learning book. I was proud that I had finished the first two and was ready for this one.

When I opened it, I saw there were drawings inside and longer words than my other books. There was a drawing of a school and another drawing of a large wagon. And there was a drawing of something I had seen before in He Sapa. The cousins had built it so we could walk over the top of a creek rather than having to wade through its cold swirling water.

This thing in the drawing crossed over a rushing river that looked very dangerous. A white man and child stood on one side and were waving to a woman and child to cross from the other. The letters below were *b-r-i-d-g-e*.

Walks Tall came into the room.

"Walks Tall," I asked, showing her the drawing. "What is this word? How do you say it?"

"It's a bridge," she said. "This says a bridge can help you get from one place to another safely."

I kept thinking about this bridge all through evening meal and bedtime prayers. When the lights were put out, I pulled the learning book from beneath my pillow and went to the window space so I could see by the moon's light.

There was something important about this bridge drawing, about getting from one place to another safely. I thought about the time I had spent trying to understand the rules of the white world at the school. I had spent much time wondering why I had been sent and what my purpose was supposed to be.

We live in the white world, Uncle had said.

We need your help, Father had added.

And then I understood what Uncle had meant. He had sent me to be a kind of bridge for my tiospaye.

I could bring my tiospaye understanding of the white man's world. I could help my people understand the ways whites used stick marks for words and clocks for telling the time of day. I could help my people walk the bridge the whites were building for me at the school.

I felt so excited by this new realization I could hardly sleep that night. I would work hard and make Miss Beatrice proud of the bridges I was building. I would make my tiospaye proud. It was my purpose.

SEVEN
DANCE

The next afternoon, Pinch Finger gathered us together.

"'Tonight Miss Beatrice will host a bonfire for you," she announced. "Ella, go find some long sticks to use for roasting. Anna, get some kindling from the bushes."

She looked around. "I don't know where William is, but we need wood. Sarah," she said to me, "you can get wood. It's there." She pointed in the direction of the barn, where large piles of wood were stacked against a wall.

I walked toward the barn cautiously, knowing this was where the boy stayed. I was more afraid of him than of the white god. The white god had done nothing to me. But the boy William had burned my clothes.

As I got closer to the woodpile I could see several knotholes in the barn's wall. Movement from inside caught my eye, and I pressed against one of the holes and peered inside. The movement was coming from William. He was dancing.

His steps were loose and graceful and looked nothing like the boy who stumbled and walked around in a daze. His arms moved fluidly, and I could almost hear the sound of the elders' drums as he danced in time to a silent beat.

It reminded me of the way Cousin had danced. Her long legs had been graceful and her body had been vibrant, even with hunger. I ached for the dance I loved.

Suddenly the boy stopped and looked in my direction. Had he seen me? Frightened, I grabbed several pieces of wood and ran toward the house, not looking back.

❊ ❊ ❊

That night stars dotted the sky, and it was almost chilly enough to need a shawl. The other girls laughed and talked, but I watched William as he made the fire.

He had changed from the boy I had seen in the barn. Rather than graceful, he was slow and awkward as he stacked the wood. I noticed that one hand was badly scarred, the skin pulled tightly against his fingers.

It took him several tries but finally he was able to light the fire before shuffling awkwardly back to the barn. The flames crackled and danced, spitting sparks into the air.

Miss Beatrice walked around, giving each of us a small handful of dough from a basket.

"Take the dough like this," she said, showing us how to twist it around a stick. "Then put it in the fire."

I played with the dough in my fingers. It felt nothing like the wasna and dried foods I was used to. It was smooth but easy to squish in my palm.

I wrapped my dough around a stick and placed it above the flames. Slowly, it turned a golden brown and began to look like the bread I had grown used to eating. I smiled. I hadn't known that bread started as this dough.

Miss Beatrice sat down with us.

"I love watching the fire," she said. "The way the flames move and spark. They bring light and then go out at the same time."

"It makes me think of lightning," I said, "how it can be so hot that it can start a fire."

"It makes me think of the dance, of the last time I danced

with my cousins," Walks Tall said dreamily.

I nodded, thinking again of the boy William in the barn and how much I missed watching Cousin dance.

Without speaking, Walks Tall stood and began dancing with small, light steps. I stared at her, and then looked at Miss Beatrice, knowing that dancing was something that was forbidden.

But Miss Beatrice said nothing. She stood and turned away from us, tending the fire, pretending as if she didn't know what was happening behind her.

Walks Tall finished her short dance, and Moon Awake stood, completing her own quick dance.

The fire popped, making a kind of drumbeat.

No one else stood. No one else danced. Walks Tall and Moon Awake had said enough for all of us, even though no words had been spoken.

EIGHT

TRUTH

At morning meal the next day, Miss Beatrice's eyes looked puffy, as if she had been crying.

Pinch Finger stood in a corner with her arms crossed, watching us.

"Children." Miss Beatrice was unsmiling. "Stand for prayers."

Small Rose stood and elbowed the person next to her, who elbowed back. Both girls giggled.

"That is not the way good Christian children behave," Miss Beatrice snapped. "That is the behavior of savages."

I stared at Miss Beatrice. I had never heard her use that word.

We finished the meal quickly and quietly.

"Did you hear about Miss Beatrice?" Moon Awake walked next to me as we went to the schoolhouse.

"What about her?" I asked.

"She got in trouble with Miss Agnes, with Pinch Finger. Pinch Finger saw us dancing last night when we were with Miss Beatrice and Miss Beatrice didn't stop us. So now she's in trouble."

"How do you know this?" I asked. Moon Awake always seemed to know things that were going on with the teachers, things that no one else did.

"I heard them last night, when I went to use the privy," she said, smiling. Moon Awake could be absolutely silent in her movements. She would have been a good hunter.

In the schoolroom, I noticed that Pinch Finger was in the room, standing in the back.

Miss Beatrice began with a history lesson, one of her favorite subjects to teach.

During history she would teach about the white leaders called the presidents. In her teaching I had come to understand they were important chiefs, with many warriors who followed them.

But she was even impatient during the history lesson.

"Who was our first president?" Miss Beatrice asked.

Walks Tall stood and answered, "George Washington."

"Correct! And what were the years of his presidency?"

Walks Tall faltered.

"Anna," she said to Walks Tall, "you must study more if you want to be educated."

I had been studying. I knew the answer, and I wanted to show Miss Beatrice that I was learning what was important to her.

I stood.

"Sarah?" Miss Beatrice pointed to me.

"Seventeen eighty-nine to seventeen ninety-seven," I said.

"Correct! Sarah, you know the presidents well!"

I smiled proudly.

A bang sounded behind me, making us all jump. I turned to see a book lying upside down on the floor near the boy William.

"William!" Miss Beatrice said. "You—"

"Pick up that book!" Pinch Finger snapped, interrupting Miss Beatrice.

But instead of doing as he was told, the boy took Small Rose's book from her desk and dropped it upside down on the floor. He went to someone else and did the same thing with another book.

"That is enough, William!" Pinch Finger said. "To the front."

No one moved as he slowly shuffled toward her. I knew what was going to happen, but I didn't want to see it.

"I know you don't always understand things, William," Pinch Finger said, speaking slowly and loudly. "But you must learn to be civilized. You must learn to treat your books with respect."

Miss Beatrice stood frozen nearby, the teaching stick still in her hands.

Taking the stick from Miss Beatrice, Pinch Finger took William's hands, turned them palm side up, and gave each palm five sharp strikes with the stick. I winced with each crack.

But the boy just stared straight at her, not looking down respectfully as he should with an elder, but staring right into her eyes. He did not flinch as the ruler struck his hands.

"Now sit down and act like a civilized young man," Pinch Finger finished. Then she turned to Miss Beatrice and said, "That is how you rid them of savagery."

The rest of the morning passed in almost complete

silence. Miss Beatrice finished her lesson, and we all huddled over our readers. No one spoke. No one looked at anyone else. I just wanted the morning to finish without anyone else getting hit.

✵ ✵ ✵

With the clang of the lunch meal bell, I stood, relieved that I could escape the room for a little while. The air was chilly, but I wanted to get away from the teachers. I joined Walks Tall and Moon Awake at our usual place by the big tree near the school yard. We sat eating quietly, our thoughts filled with the morning's events.

A shadow appeared, and I looked up to see William standing in front of me.

"You admire the Great White Fathers?" he asked in perfect Lakota.

I looked at him. His voice was strong. His eyes looked angry.

Walks Tall glared at him. "We're trying to eat, William," she said slowly, so that he would understand her white words.

"You admire the Great White Fathers?" he repeated, still looking at me.

"No," I said, standing. "I hate the Great White Father!" I could feel my face grow warm.

"But you know their names, their dates," he continued in Lakota. "You enjoy learning about the Great White Fathers."

His words were pointed, intended to shoot like an arrow.

Anger flashed, burning hot. Who was this boy with his short hair who had burned my clothes? Who was this slow boy to question me about the presidents?

"I hate the Great White Father," I repeated. "He is the one who breaks all his promises. He is the one who lets us starve!"

"And yet you answer every question about the Great White Fathers correctly," he continued calmly.

"Those are the *presidents*, not the Great White Father," I said, trying to keep control of my anger.

"The presidents *are* the Great White Fathers," he spat out. Then he turned and walked away.

I watched him leave, unable to believe what he had just said. I knew he was slow. Surely, he was confused about the presidents, the leaders Miss Beatrice admired so much. I was certain the president wasn't the Great White Father.

"Walks Tall," I asked, "is this true? Are the presidents the same as the Great White Father?"

"Oh, Four Winds," she said. "He is slow. And I already told you that you should not talk to him. He is trouble."

"But . . ."

"He is right. They *are* the same," Moon Awake said. "The president is what the whites call him, but my tiospaye calls him the Great White Father."

"Oh," I said, suddenly feeling sick. The boy's arrow had hit its target.

✼ ✼ ✼

That night I lay in the dark, wrestling with this new truth, longing for the presence of the elders of my tiospaye. I wanted to speak with Uncle. I knew he would listen as I talked, letting me speak until all the words were out. Then he would think in his quiet way and offer wisdom. I wondered what his advice would be about this new truth I had uncovered.

But even when I tried to imagine his voice, all I could hear were the whisperings of the girls around me and the rattling of confused thoughts in my head.

I thought of the beatings at the school and the rules I didn't understand. I thought of the white god and the Jesus and never being able to say my real name or speak in my real language. I thought of being a savage and being uncivilized.

And I began to have a new understanding.

The teachers at the school didn't want to help my people. They weren't interested in building bridges. I thought I understood why Uncle had sent me, to be a bridge. But the whites didn't want a bridge.

NINE
PUNISHMENT

After several days, Pinch Finger finally stopped following Miss Beatrice everywhere, and Miss Beatrice seemed happier.

"Today we have a surprise for you," she announced one afternoon after our meal break. "This afternoon, instead of lessons, we will sew."

My heart fluttered with excitement. Not long before, I had learned that the white word for sewing was something like the beading I did with Mother.

As a young child, I had spent hours watching Mother grow pictures beneath her fingers with beads. She had spent years teaching me what she knew. Someday I hoped to be as skilled as she was in both beading and quillwork. But since coming to the school, I had not been allowed to do either. I hoped I remembered how.

Miss Beatrice placed small baskets of beads on a table and began to hand out needles and thread, humming softly as she did this.

"Take this, Sarah," she said, handing me a needle. "Be careful with it. Don't poke yourself."

I studied the metal needle. I had only worked with needles made of bone. This one was smaller and didn't feel as if it fit my fingers. But it didn't matter. I was so excited to bead that I knew I could learn how to use it.

"Oh, not you, William," I heard Miss Beatrice say. "This is women's work. Brother Huber is here today to fix the roof. You will help him. We need to get the roof ready for winter."

I glanced over to see William slouching in his usual way. He had been correct about the presidents and the Great White Father, and for some reason this made me angry. How could a boy so slow be wise enough to know this? And how could I not have known this? I realized I was more angry with myself than with him.

I shook the anger away, looking back at the needle and thread, imagining what kind of patterns I could make. I would create a star, something small that I could give Bear.

"And here is the best part, children." Miss Beatrice unrolled a long piece of cloth that the whites called burlap. "Won't it be grand?" she asked.

"What is that?" Moon Awake whispered to me.

I shrugged. I had never seen burlap close up before, and it was cut in such a long strip.

"What is it?" Walks Tall asked.

"It's a banner!" Miss Beatrice said. "Come closer." She beckoned to us to gather around.

"There is the name of our school." She pointed to words I could see outlined faintly in chalk. ALL SAINTS MISSIONARY SCHOOL.

"Brother Huber has arranged for a photograph to be taken. Isn't that grand? A photograph! It will be our first, so we want to make sure that everyone knows the name of this special place, of our special school.

"You will outline the words with pretty colors of thread so we can read it. It is called embroidery. I found a few beads you can add too. Not many, but they will do."

Miss Beatrice laid the banner out on the floor and looked at us expectantly.

"Now come find a place and start working, girls."

I stared at the banner, not wanting to find a place to work. I wanted to bead as I had with my mother. I didn't want to do this embroidery. I didn't want to help make a banner of white words with a metal needle.

"Sit here. Next to me." Walks Tall pulled at my sleeve. "It will be fun," she said.

I sighed and sat down.

"At least we don't have to do lessons," she whispered.

"Oh, but I forgot scissors," Miss Beatrice exclaimed. "They are in the office. Sarah, Anna, will you get them, please? They are on the desk."

"Yes, Miss Beatrice," Walks Tall answered, and led me out of the school.

"What is an office?" I asked as we walked through the church into a room to the side.

"This," she said.

I looked around, fascinated. Inside the small room were a desk and a wooden chair and many bookshelves filled with books. I didn't know there could be so many books in one place.

"What are you girls doing?" Miss Margaret was in the doorway, frowning. "You shouldn't be alone here."

"Miss Beatrice asked us to bring scissors," Walks Tall answered, looking respectfully down at the floor.

"There are so many books," I murmured.

"Yes," Miss Margaret said, her manner brightening. "Knowledge is the foundation of learning."

"And who is that?" I asked, pointing to the picture of a woman who had a circle of light around her head.

"That is Mary, the mother of Jesus," Miss Margaret said. "We've talked about this in church lessons."

I did remember hearing about the mother of the Jesus, but I had never seen a picture of her. She looked sad. Was it because someone was hurting her son?

I continued to look around, pleased that I could read so many of the white words that were on books and pictures. But when I got to a small sign hanging above the desk, I froze.

I read the words carefully, and then read them again. The wooden sign was small, but the letters were large, simple, and clear.

KILL THE INDIAN, SAVE THE MAN.

I read it again. KILL THE INDIAN, SAVE THE MAN.

I couldn't look away.

"That is a very special plaque," Miss Margaret said, noticing that I was staring. "Colonel Pratt gave it to us.

Miss Agnes and I had the chance to visit his school. It is similar to ours although his is much bigger. He is such an inspiration, a true inspiration."

"But what does it mean?" I whispered.

Kill the Indian. I couldn't stop staring.

"It means that to be civilized you cannot be a savage," Miss Margaret explained. "You must get rid of the savage so you can fit into society."

I could only stare, feeling angry and confused.

"Is there trouble, girls? What's taking so long?" Miss Beatrice's voice sounded from behind.

"You shouldn't have let these girls in here by themselves," Miss Margaret was saying. "Who knows what kind of trouble they could have caused?"

My anger exploded and I reached for the plaque, ripping it down from the wall and breaking it over my knee.

"What are you doing?" Miss Margaret screeched, jumping toward me. "Stop!"

"Sarah, stop!" Miss Beatrice said, reaching for the plaque.

I looked down and realized I was still holding its broken pieces, and I threw them to the floor.

"Miss Margaret, what is going on here?" Pastor Huber had appeared.

"My plaque. My plaque," she sobbed.

Walks Tall had disappeared from the room.

"I told you not to let those heathen children back here," Pastor Huber said, and he grabbed my arm, yanking hard, pulling me out of the office. A belt appeared, and he began hitting me wherever he could reach, spitting words out between the hard thwacks.

"Will teach you, you little savage . . . Think it's just natural to break anything. And from someone who was trying to help you!"

My skin burned. But I would not cry. I would stare straight ahead with dignity.

"You can just sit in here and think about what you have done," Pastor Huber finally said, dragging me into a small darkened room. The cloaks he wore during the church service hung limply along the wall.

". . . heathen children."

He was still muttering as he locked the door.

I curled into a corner and hugged my knees to my chest. Places on my arms stung and my legs hurt. I wished for Cousin to be locked in the closet with me. If she were with me, I knew she would find a way to make me feel better. I closed my eyes and imagined the sound of her voice. I pretended that she was sitting right next to me and I was not completely alone.

✿ ✿ ✿

It felt like hours later when I heard the sound of a lock turning in the door. Light flooded in, hurting my eyes. Once they adjusted, I could see Miss Margaret and Pastor Huber peering in. I had been crouched on the floor so long it was difficult to stand.

Pastor Huber reached in and pulled me out by an arm. It hurt where he touched me, but I didn't cry out.

Miss Margaret looked at me and gasped. There was a small trickle of blood on one arm from where I had been hit with the belt. An angry bruise was blossoming on my other arm.

"Sarah, I hope you have learned your lesson," Pastor Huber said.

I looked him in the eye. I would not look down at the floor. I said nothing.

"You will apologize to Miss Margaret," he thundered.

"Miss Margaret," I said, "I am sorry."

But I wasn't sorry. I wished the plaque could be added

to the same fire the boy William had used to burn my clothing.

"Oh, Sarah," was all Miss Margaret said. She reached toward me, and I flinched. "Oh, Sarah," she repeated.

※ ※ ※

I went straight to our sleeping room without dinner and lay down on my sleeping space. The girls arrived later, walking in quietly as if I was sick.

"Four Winds?" Walks Tall said, coming to my side.

When I didn't respond, she sat down, patting me lightly on my back.

I didn't move as the other girls changed into nightclothes. Miss Beatrice came for night prayers, and I stayed on my sleeping space, my back turned away from her. No one insisted that I join them.

The lanterns were blown out, and I turned to find the moon through the window space.

TEN
RUNNING

I lay silently until I was sure everyone was asleep, thoughts racing through my mind.

Not so long ago I had been sure of my purpose, certain I was meant to be a bridge for my people. Now I could see I had been terribly wrong.

Kill the Indian, save the man.

The teachers at the school didn't want me to help my people. They didn't want my people to exist at all.

I knew I could no longer stay.

I arose quietly and looked around.

I watched Walks Tall sleeping peacefully, trying to decide if I should wake her. I wanted to beg her to come with me.

I didn't want to leave her behind. But in my heart I knew this was my journey and I had to take it alone.

"Be well," I whispered. Then I gathered my clothes and crept down the stairs to the pantry.

I would pack food for two days' travel. By wagon, it had taken one day to reach the school. I thought it would take two days to walk back to my tiospaye.

I took several muffins from a basket and found hard-boiled eggs. I took two and tucked it all inside a folded square of cloth. I had gone without food many times. I could miss meals if I had to.

"What are you doing?"

I heard the whisper before I saw Moon Awake.

"I . . . I'm . . . ," I stuttered.

"Are you leaving? Are you running away?" She stepped into the stream of moonlight shining in from the window near the pantry.

"Yes," I said, trying to sound braver than I felt.

She studied me, her eyes traveling over my clothes and the small bundle of food I had packed.

"They will bring you back," she said. "Others have run. And they have been brought back. It is foolish to run. It will only make things worse." Her words sounded harsh, but I could see softness in her eyes.

"You can come with me," I said. "We can go together."

For a moment, I thought she was going to agree. I thought she was going to pack her own bundle of food and follow me.

But she shook her head no.

"I can't stay," I said, trying to let those simple words explain everything.

"And I can't go," Moon Awake answered with a catch in her voice, as if she were going to cry. She touched my hand, then moved silently back into the dark.

I crept outside into the cool of the night and stood shivering, wondering if my decision had been correct. I was not afraid of the travel. I had spent my childhood walking with our tiospaye from our He Sapa summer camp to our winter camp near the big rock. That journey had taken what the whites called weeks. We had had to set up camp and spend nights beneath the stars. I had learned about finding water and searching for food in the wild grasses and plants.

But this was different. This was not traveling with my tiospaye, moving as one with the moons. This was running. And it was running away from something I had been sent to by our elders.

I had never defied anyone in this manner. Even though I was too quick to anger at times, I had always respected the wisdom of the elders. What would they think when I returned?

I thought of a young warrior in our tiospaye who had fought with another and killed him in anger. The warrior's punishment had been banishment. He had been forced to leave our tiospaye, and no one had heard of him again.

What if I was turned away, banished from my tiospaye? What would happen to me? I would prefer death to being ignored by my family and my little brother. Tears sprang to my eyes at the thought of this.

Courage, I could hear Cousin whisper.

I looked up into the sky, noticing the vast number of stars. I scanned the blackness, searching for one bright star, the polestar.

Do you see? I thought of Uncle telling me about the polestar. I could see his hand pointing up to the stars, moving until he was pointing at one of the brightest. I could hear his voice, quiet, strong, and steady.

Do you see, Niece?

It is a star, Uncle, I had said impatiently when I was very young. I didn't understand why this star was different.

It is special, he continued. *It is the polestar. All the other stars in the sky move as the night continues. But this star stays in one place as the other stars dance around it in celebration. No matter where you are, you will always know how to find your way if you can see the polestar.*

I swallowed hard, imagining the sad look on Uncle's face if he was disappointed that I had returned. I looked back at the school. I could easily return, crawl back into bed, and continue to try to learn the ways of the whites.

But then I looked at the bruise on my arm. Kill the Indian, save the man.

No. I could not stay.

I looked back up at the polestar. It would be my guide back to my tiospaye.

"You will need these."

I stifled a scream at the sound of the voice and whirled around to see William standing behind me.

"What are you doing here?" I whispered.

"You will need these," he repeated, holding out his hand. "For your journey."

In the moonlight I could see Bear's small carved rabbit and Mother's wotawe in his open palm.

I gasped. "How did you get these? You burned them!"

He put them in my hand. "I took them before I threw your clothes into the fire. I knew they were important. I would never burn these sacred things."

I stood staring at him, too surprised to say anything, tears welling in my eyes. "Thank you," I managed to say.

He turned and walked toward the school.

I watched him take long strides across the field. He was not walking with his usual shuffle, but rather standing tall and straight, moving with purpose.

I slipped the wotawe over my head and squeezed the rabbit. Then I turned and began to walk in the direction the polestar pointed.

ELEVEN

JOURNEY

I walked until the polestar disappeared and the early rays of the sun appeared. I would travel beneath the cover of night and sleep during the day. My hope was that I had already traveled far before anyone would discover I was missing.

In the early light, I could see outcroppings of distant jagged cliffs. The teachers at the school called these cliffs the badlands. But to my people they were Makoce Sica.

Cousin and I had been frightened of these cliffs. Legend said this was the place where the bones of Unktehi, the Water Monster, rested. Some said they could still feel her moving there, waiting to knock the cliffs over on people foolish enough to venture inside the valleys of stone.

But this time seeing the cliffs brought me comfort instead of fear. Their appearance meant I was getting closer to my tiospaye.

I found a small grove of trees and put down my pack. Carefully, I made a hiding place out of branches and crawled inside. I opened my bundle and nibbled one of the muffins. I could feel the chill of the air reaching through my clothes, and I wrapped myself inside the blanket I had taken from my bed. Suddenly I was so exhausted I could barely keep my eyes open.

I rubbed Mother's wotawe gently, feeling strengthened, and fell asleep.

✲ ✲ ✲

I awoke to the sounds of coyotes calling to one another in the dark.

"Run on! Run on!" they seemed to say, and I felt renewed courage from their voices.

My feet had grown numb in the pinchy shoes I was still wearing. My legs felt stiff and sore as I continued to walk. Even though I had slept soundly, I felt tired and achy.

I thought of my family to distract me from my tired body.

I could picture Bear running through the grasses, his

restless spirit in constant need of motion. There had been times I had grown tired of his endless questions. How I looked forward to those questions now.

Mother would be getting ready for the winter moons. She would be preparing thread and needle to mend clothing and sleeping skins and other things in need of repair. I would join her in this work, using the bone needles I was used to, not the metal needles the whites used. And I would bead in the traditional way and Mother would be proud of my work.

Father would be with the scouts, trying to find game to dry for the winter moons. If they were lucky, they might find a deer or antelope and provide more food for our tiospaye than the meager rations we received.

Uncle would be meeting with the elders in the council lodge. They would discuss the important happenings in our tiospaye. They would discuss the future and share stories of the past.

But then, like an angry thief, memories of the school would start to take over my thoughts.

Kill the Indian. Savage. Cut hair. Beatings.

Instead I focused on the polestar to clear my head, or studied Makoce Sica, cutting jagged outlines into the night.

I searched the sky for other star pictures and kept walking

the path that seemed to stretch forever.

And finally, as the sun began to appear in the sky, I saw the faint image of tipis in the distance.

I stumbled as I quickened my pace, wanting to run to my family. But my people were still far away, and my body ached too much to run.

Bear was playing outside with the cousins, and when I saw him, I did begin to run.

"Little Brother!" I called when I was close enough to be heard.

"Sister!" he cried. He sprinted toward me but then came to a sudden stop.

"Sister, your clothes," he whispered, his eyes large. "Your hair."

"Bear, it is me!" I cried, holding my arms out to him, wanting desperately to touch him.

He shook his head, and I could see fear in his eyes.

"Bear, it is Sister," I said. My heart felt as if it might break. "I have the rabbit you made. Here it is." I showed him the small carving. "It has brought me back to you!"

He took it and rubbed it.

"Mother! Mother!" he called, dropping the rabbit and running into the tipi.

I bent down and picked up the small wooden animal, trying to stop the trembling and ignore the fear that my decision to run had been the wrong one.

Several of the young cousins stood some distance away, peering at me with wide eyes.

I looked down at my white clothes, realizing what they were seeing, a white girl in the midst of their tiospaye. I wanted to rip off my clothes and pull my hair down to make it longer again.

"Daughter!" Mother emerged from our tipi flap, and I was in her arms, clinging to her.

"Forgive me, Mother. Forgive me, please!" I said over and over again as she stroked my hair.

"Daughter," she said, touching one of the yellowing bruises on my arm. "You have been injured."

"I am home, Mother," I said. "I am safe now."

She led me inside our tipi, and I stood breathing in the familiar scent of my home. My eyes wandered over things I had not seen for so long; the cooking pot hanging, the sleeping skins rolled up neatly for the day, Mother's necessary bag on a small post.

I started crying and couldn't stop, feeling all of the fear and exhaustion pouring out of me.

"Rest. Rest, Daughter," Mother said, going to the cooking fire and bringing me a warm drink. She bent down and unrolled the sleeping skins across the place I used to sleep.

"Shhh," she said, covering me with soft skins after I had finished drinking. Easily, I fell asleep.

I awoke as Father and Uncle returned in the late afternoon. Mother greeted them first, speaking in hushed tones. I stood by my sleeping skins, looking down, waiting to be addressed.

"Daughter," Father said, and Uncle nodded.

"Father!" I cried. "Uncle! Forgive me, please forgive me! I have failed," I said quietly.

Uncle held up his hand. "We eat," he said.

❈ ❈ ❈

Our meal was more plentiful than before I had been taken away. There was soup as always, watery, with a few vegetables. But there was some meat, enough so that we could each have a mouthful. I hoped Mother hadn't used special reserves because of my return. I hoped they had not sacrificed because of me.

When the meal finished, I helped Mother gather the skin bowls and we all sat together as a family. The quiet felt strange. I had grown used to the constant noise of other girls. The quiet of my own family felt unfamiliar.

Uncle spoke.

"Tell us of your journey," he said.

The story tumbled out of me in a rush of words I hadn't realized was inside. I started at the beginning, with my arrival at the school and the strangeness of everything. I told of the way white people give names freely and that I was not allowed to speak Lakota or say my Lakota name. I spoke of the teachers and the pastor and of trying to learn to be civilized.

I explained how lost and confused I had felt at first until I learned about the word "bridge." And how I had thought I was meant to help build bridges between our people and the whites. But then I had discovered that the teachers at the school weren't interested in bridges.

I told of learning that the Great White Father was the president and that everything that was important to me was wrong at the school and that I was called a savage.

In a whisper, I told them of the banner Miss Beatrice had unrolled for us, and of being asked to get the scissors from the office.

"I wanted to see this office because I had never seen

one," I said, feeling ashamed to remember how excited I had been.

"There were many books and I felt pride to know I could read much of what was there. I had learned many white words. But on the wall there was a small wooden sign." I stopped, looking down, not wanting to continue.

"The sign was a treasure of Miss Margaret," I said quietly, starting to cry. "And it said, 'Kill the Indian, save the man.' "

Mother gasped.

"I have tried not to let my anger strike like lightning. I really have," I said, too ashamed to look at my family. "But I was so angry and I couldn't control it and I grabbed the sign and I broke it." I looked down at the bruise on my arm. "And I was punished."

I paused momentarily, waiting until I had control of my tears.

". . . and that was when I realized I could not stay, when I realized the teachers were not interested in helping to build a bridge."

Finally there was nothing more left to tell and I leaned back, exhausted. I was relieved to have told my story but afraid of what Uncle and Father would say.

"We will discuss this," Uncle said, looking over at Father.

"And we will talk more after that. For now, you must rest, Niece."

There was no more speaking then, no more words that needed to be said. Quietly, I crawled beneath my sleeping skins. Even though my head was full of doubt and fear, it was as if I had never left. I was home.

Mother came to me and sat, stroking my hair.

"I am sorry they cut my hair, Mother," I whispered. "I tried to stop them, but I couldn't."

"Hush now. It is time to sleep," she whispered back.

I nodded and fell asleep to the comforting sounds of my family around me.

TWELVE
HOME

There were no bells clanging the next morning. Instead, I awoke to the sounds of birds calling on the prairie and the quiet sounds of Mother moving nearby.

"Where is Uncle?" I asked. "And Father?"

"They meet with the elders at the council lodge. Here," Mother said, handing me a deerskin dress to wear.

I took the dress and held it close to my face, feeling its softness against my skin. Eagerly, I slipped it on.

"One of the cousins brought these for you." She handed me a pair of moccasins, and I put them on my feet. I wiggled my toes, happy that I could once again wear comfortable foot coverings.

"Let's burn this," I said, holding up the dress I had been wearing. "And these," I added, picking up the hard shoes.

She looked at me strangely, but followed me outside.

We walked some distance from our tipi and cleared a circle for a fire. Several nights of frost had put most of the prairie plants to sleep as they prepared for the upcoming winter moons. Soon the entire prairie would be covered with snow. I had always loved the time of the new snow, when the world would be painted in soft whiteness.

We built a fire, and I tossed the clothes and shoes on the flames, watching with satisfaction as they burned.

"There was one boy at the school," I said, remembering how I had watched William throw my clothes into the fire.

"I forgot to speak of him yesterday," I said. "When I first came to the school, the teachers took my clothes and he burned them."

I pulled the cord up that held my wotawe and let it hang outside my dress. "And I thought he burned this too. But he saved it from the fire. He gave it back to me."

I thought of his slow walk and stooped shoulders and the way I had seen him dance in the barn with such grace.

"Everyone calls this boy slow," I said, "but I don't think he is slow. He is a mystery."

"A mystery," Mother repeated. Then she said, "There are other mysteries. Some you will understand and some you will not."

I wasn't used to hearing my mother talk this way.

"What do you mean?" I asked.

"You spoke of bridges and of wondering why the elders would send you to this place."

I nodded.

"We did not let you go by choice," she said quietly.

I stared at her.

"What do you mean?" I asked.

"When the whites in their wagon came, the agency had already told them of our children. You were the right age and female, what they needed for their girls' school. They want to show the Great White Father what they are doing in their schools, and they needed more students."

I stared at her.

"They told us we must send you or they would withhold our rations."

I felt numb. My being at the school had never been about bridges. It had been about food and nothing else. That was how I had helped my tiospaye. I had saved them from starvation.

"I should not tell you this." Mother did not look at me. "It would cause Uncle shame. Do you understand?"

"Yes, Mother," I said, and touched her hand. She looked up at me, and I saw tears in her eyes.

"It is good that I know," I said.

Later that day, Uncle and Father returned to our tipi. I waited for them to talk with me, to tell me their thoughts on my decision. But without saying anything, they took arrows and bows and left.

"Mother, what do you think was decided?" I asked.

I could hardly keep from running after them and begging to know what had happened in the council lodge. Had I caused shame? Would I be allowed to stay?

"We wait, Daughter," she said. "Until they are ready to speak."

"But—" I said, and she turned away from me, ending our talk.

I helped prepare the evening meal in silence, chopping the few greens that had been dried. Mother took several handfuls of dried corn from a basket and added them to the boiling water.

I could hear her words echo in my head. *We did not let you go by choice. They told us they would withhold our rations.*

Soon enough Father and Uncle returned with a small rabbit. Mother and I prepared the rabbit and added part of it to the stew, preparing the rest to dry. Then we sat and ate as a family.

I waited for Father or Uncle to speak first, growing more anxious as each moment of silence passed.

"And now we talk," Uncle finally said, and I felt my stomach clench with fear.

"Your choice to run was difficult," Father began.

I nodded. It had been difficult.

"But there were reasons behind this running, reasons that you explained, that we understand."

"I couldn't stay. I had to run," I agreed.

"Your decision to leave was a wise one," Uncle said.

I looked up, surprised.

"Sometimes you have to stay," he continued. "And sometimes you have to run. It takes courage to know the difference."

"Courage," I repeated, finding my voice.

"Courage," Uncle said again.

Slowly, I realized I was not going to be forced to leave. I had not brought shame to my tiospaye. The elders respected my decision.

Later that evening Bear curled up on his sleeping skins, and I joined him. "This is so special to me, Brother," I said, making his small wooden rabbit hop down one of his legs.

"Sister?" he asked.

"Yes?"

"Why did you cut your hair?" He reached out and touched my hair.

"I was not given a choice," I answered.

His eyes widened. "The whites sound fierce."

"They say we are savages," I said, looking down at one of the bruises on my arm. "But I think they are the savage ones."

He nodded, saying nothing more.

THIRTEEN

DECISION

That night I dreamt of Cousin. We stood together on a ridge in the forest of He Sapa. Sheer rock dropped beneath us into a valley below. Around us tall pine trees reached into the sky like fingers.

I could feel the earth on my bare toes and the warmth of the sun on my face. The wind began as a small breeze until it swelled into a chain of whispers passing from one tree to the next.

"Cousin," I said. "The trees speak. Listen."

We both stood quietly until the wind moved to another part of the forest.

"What was the message?" she asked.

"Our ancestors say three things," I answered. *"Strength. Courage. Respect."*

"Those are good things," she said.

"Yes." I nodded, and turned to embrace her. But she was gone.

When I awoke, it was cold in our tipi. The fire was not yet lit, and I lay shivering beneath my sleeping skins. I could hear the wind blowing on the prairie, but it sounded different from the wind in my dream. There was something familiar in the sound, but at first I didn't know what it was.

Then I sat upright, realizing what the sound was.

"A wagon. A wagon." Bear dashed in through the tipi flap, confirming what I feared.

I jumped up and followed him outside.

From a distance, I could see a cloud of dust approaching. My stomach dropped. It was a white wagon.

"Inside," I said, grabbing Bear by the hand, pulling him back into our tipi with me. Suddenly I wanted to run to safety, take Bear with me, get away from the whites and their wagon and their school.

Mother came in with the day's water she had drawn from the pump.

"I'll find someone to get Father and Uncle," she said, hurrying back out.

As the wagon pulled to a stop near our tipi, I peeked out through the tipi flap. Pinch Finger sat in the wagon, along with Pastor Huber and an agency official.

I felt sick.

". . . in the council lodge." One of the uncles was trying to get them to meet in the council lodge.

"No! We have come for Sarah. She will return with us," the agency official translated for the uncle.

I didn't need a translation. I could understand their angry white words on my own.

Father and Uncle appeared, and Pastor Huber stepped toward them.

"We have come for Sarah. She must return to school. You know what will happen if she does not."

I swallowed, knowing he was talking about the rations.

"Sarah? Sarah?" Uncle said after the words had been translated. "There is no Sarah here."

"I don't know what her *Indian* name is," the pastor said, spitting out the word *Indian* as if it were a rattlesnake inside his mouth.

I stepped from behind the tipi flap and stood as tall as I could.

"Sarah," Pinch Finger said. "Stop this foolishness."

"Not Sarah!" Uncle yelled, using the white words. Then more quietly, in Lakota, he said, "There is only this girl." He pointed to me. "Four Winds."

Now Uncle spoke to me. "Four Winds, go back inside. We will settle this."

I thought of the few mouthfuls of meat that had been added to our meal and the flour rations Mother had just begun to receive. If I stayed, the whites would withhold rations. If I stayed, my family would starve.

"No," I said quietly in Lakota. "I will return." The agency official translated from my side.

"That is *exactly* what is going to happen," Pastor Huber said, throwing an angry glance at Uncle.

"Four Winds, it is your decision. If you choose to stay, we will fight," Uncle whispered.

"I must return," I said.

He nodded.

I could hear Cousin's voice in the prairie wind.

Courage, she whispered.

I pushed my tears away, gathering strength.

I would return to being the white Indian girl. I would not be a bridge, because I knew there were no bridges being built. I would return to keep my family from starving.

I felt nothing as I was loaded into the whites' wagon once again. Mother hugged me, and I could feel her trembling. She pointed to where she knew the wotawe hung around my neck beneath my dress. I nodded back, clutching Bear's wooden rabbit in my palm. I knew how to keep them safe this time. They would not get burned.

☼☼☼

It was dark when we arrived at the school. Once again I followed Pinch Finger inside the building and up the stairs into the sleeping room where the other girls were. Prayers had already been said, and the girls were in their sleeping spaces.

Once again, I could see white clothes laid out on my sleeping space for me.

". . . just pretend like this unfortunate incident never happened," Pinch Finger said. I heard the words but wasn't listening.

". . . a good thing that the snow has not fallen yet. My goodness, Sarah, you could have been hurt."

"My name is not Sarah," I said quietly, using the white words.

She stopped talking, a surprised look on her face.

"You do remember the language. I was afraid you had forgotten," she said, an air of relief in her voice.

"My name is Four Winds," I said. "Not Sarah."

She peered at me.

I gritted my teeth, preparing to be slapped for saying my Lakota name. I stared at her defiantly. I was stronger than her slaps, stronger than anything she could do to me.

"It is time for prayers and bed," she said.

I pulled my deerskin dress over my head and took the wotawe from my neck, slipping it and the rabbit beneath my pillow. Pinch Finger turned to leave.

"Wait," I said. "You will want to burn this." She turned back to look at me, and I handed her the dress. "It has been with the savages."

"Oh, Sarah, don't make this difficult." She took the dress and stared at me, an almost pleading look in her eyes.

I turned away from her and dressed in the white nightclothes. I climbed into my sleeping space, trying to see the moon through the window. It had long since moved with the changing of the season, and I could no longer see it from where I lay. Carefully, I pulled at the seams of my pillow to make a small hole, then I took the wooden rabbit and wotawe and tucked them safely inside.

"Four Winds," Walks Tall whispered from her space, "I am glad you are back."

I said nothing.

115

FOURTEEN
RENEWAL

My anger burned like a fire, constantly threatening to engulf me.

I was angry at the whites. I was angry at the school. And I was angry at the other girls, who did what they were told, saying the white prayers and letting their hair be cut without protest. They didn't seem to care if the Indian inside them was being killed.

I refused to talk unless directed to by a teacher. During lunch, I sat alone and nibbled at my food. During lessons, I sat in the back of the schoolroom away from everyone else.

"Four Winds," Walks Tall whispered, "why are you so angry?"

I looked at her, afraid that if I tried to answer, nothing but hurtful words would come from my mouth, words that I wouldn't be able to stop.

Moon Awake was less sympathetic.

"I told you it was a bad idea," she said. "I told you they would bring you back."

I pretended I hadn't heard her.

✻ ✻ ✻

"Sarah, please stay in the classroom after lessons," Miss Beatrice directed a few days after my return.

Obediently, I sat at my place in the back of the room as the other girls walked out for afternoon chores. William was the last to leave, and I could hear the swishing of his shoes as he shuffled out of the room with everyone else.

Miss Beatrice came and sat next to me. I refused to look at her, staring straight ahead.

"It is hard to learn new things that you do not know, to understand a different way of life," she said. "I understand it is difficult." She touched my hand.

"But there is a plan. I believe this," she continued. "And when the time is right, God reveals His plan. When I was younger, I didn't understand this, but now I see it is His plan that I teach. That I work with children. That I help you. That I help the Indians."

I looked at her and could see genuine caring in her eyes. She cared. But she knew nothing of my world. All she knew was that it should be extinguished.

I nodded, then stood and walked out.

❊ ❊ ❊

That night I knelt alongside my bed with everyone else and pretended to say prayers. I made my lips move, but no words came out. Instead of speaking the words, I thought of my little brother. He was the reason I was here. And I was the reason my tiospaye would still receive rations.

Walks Tall knelt next to me, her voice loud and clear as she repeated the white prayer. Out of the corner of my eye, I could see Moon Awake watching me. She seemed angry with me. I wasn't sure if it was because I had left or because I had returned.

The air outside had become biting cold and our sleeping room was drafty. The teachers had brought extra blankets for each of us. Snow, I knew, would soon cover the ground.

Before our confinement to the reservation, this new season had been a time of change and moving. We would gather our homes, people, and stories, and travel from the sacred He Sapa forest to the shadow of the Big Rock, where we would make our winter camp. Cousin and I would race ponies so fast across the prairie it felt as if we were the wind itself. Everything about our lives would move to the change of the seasons.

Now, nothing changed to match the moon or season or weather. Instead, things moved around the white world that rested in the middle of everything, as if it were the polestar itself.

I longed to see the moon and its steady glow. It would help soothe my anger and calm my spirit. As everyone else tried to get warm beneath their blankets, I crept to the window to try to find the moon. But when I looked out, I forgot about the moon because I saw small flakes of snow beginning to fall.

My heart lightened. Snow always did this. Even though the plants fell into slumber to prepare for its coming, the snow itself held a promise that spring would come again. I loved seeing the snow.

Movement on the ground below caught my eye, and I

blinked, not sure I could believe what I saw.

It was William. And he was dancing. Flakes of snow rested momentarily on his shoulders before dropping off in his graceful movements.

My tiospaye always danced with the first snow. We danced to celebrate the change of season and to acknowledge the movement of the earth and the moon and the harmony of both. I felt tears come to my eyes.

As I watched him I could imagine the beat of the silent drum he danced to. I could imagine the sounds of the elders' voices rising and falling in story. His dance was so clear that I could almost see the story he was telling.

I watched as long as I could, until my eyelids threatened to shut in sleep. Then I went back to my space and fell into peaceful sleep. My angry spirit had been soothed, but not by the moon. Unexpectedly, it had been soothed by William.

✵ ✵ ✵

The dull, loud clang of a bell awakened me the next morning.

"Snow!" someone cried in Lakota, and everyone ran to the small window, pushing one another to get a view. I joined from behind, looking out at the white blanket covering the ground, remembering the dance from the night before.

"It's so pretty," Walks Tall said, turning toward me. I nodded, smiling, almost forgetting my anger.

An excited hum buzzed around everyone as we ate breakfast that morning. Even Pinch Finger was smiling.

"The snow is lovely, isn't it, children?"

"Yes, Miss Agnes," everyone said in unison. I stayed silent.

"Today, after the church service, instead of reading, you will have the chance to play in the snow."

There were delighted squeals, and even I felt excited to miss our required readings on Sundays and spend time outside in the fresh new snow.

✻ ✻ ✻

"God will punish the sinners!" Pastor Huber emphasized during the service that morning. He kept looking at me as he spoke.

"Those who run from His will shall be punished!" he continued. I was sure he meant this message for me.

But I didn't care about his words. Instead, I watched William sitting a few rows ahead of me. Who was this boy who danced so gracefully and yet slouched in a slow walk and seemed to misunderstand everything?

The service ended, and we filed out of the church.

"Gather shawls and scarves, girls," Miss Margaret directed. "Get dressed for the snow!"

Pinch Finger came toward us, bundled in so many clothes she looked like an overstuffed bear. I heard a soft giggle from someone.

I turned to follow the other girls into the house when William was suddenly in front me. He stood, an unreadable expression on his face, his scarred hand resting at his side.

"You were watching me today in the church," he said in Lakota. "Why?"

He took me by surprise. I didn't know he had seen me watching him.

"I . . . I . . . ," I stuttered. I no longer felt frightened of him. But I didn't understand him and couldn't explain why.

"You what?" he hissed. "You watch to mock me?"

"No, I just . . . I miss the dance," I said quietly.

Confusion flickered across his eyes for a second and then was gone. He turned straight ahead without talking and walked toward the barn.

I watched him for a moment, then turned to join the others.

Once everyone was bundled as warmly as possible, Miss Margaret called us together in a circle. Unexpectedly, she dropped to the ground and lay on her back, moving her arms and legs in wide circles through the snow. Then she stood and pointed at the image left behind.

"Do you see, girls? It's a snow angel!" she said.

It did look like one of the spirit beings the whites called angels, with wings coming out from its sides.

"Your turn. Your turn!" she encouraged. "Try it. It is fun."

One of the younger girls started, and then we each dropped down, making snow images of the white angels. Without even realizing what we were doing, we connected our images one to the other, so that our wings formed a large circle of snow angels.

"Lovely, lovely!" Pinch Finger clapped. "Look. They're all connected like they are in heaven!"

But when I looked at the circle of images, I didn't see white angels gathered together in heaven. I saw a circle of my people dancing, their arms swaying in time to the drumbeat. I smiled to myself, realizing that in our own way, the girls of this white school had danced our Lakota dance with the first snow.

FIFTEEN
SNOW

That night I waited until everyone else was asleep and then went to the window. As my breath fogged the pane, I watched the ground below, hoping to see William dance. When he did appear, my heart jumped.

Once again his movements were so perfect I felt I could see what he was seeing and hear what he was hearing. I allowed my spirit to be taken up with his dance, to move and dream and remember along with him.

Suddenly I wanted to reclaim this piece of myself. I wanted to dance. I didn't care if I was caught and beaten again. I wanted to be brave like this boy.

I pulled on shoes and a shawl and quietly made my

way down the stairs, through the eating space, and out into the yard.

The air was colder than I had realized, and I shivered as I sat on the steps, waiting to see what William would do next.

He looked up at me briefly and then went back to his dance. Even though it was cold, he wore no shawl. He was dancing free and unrestrained.

I could see stories as he moved, and I imagined buffalo running majestic and free. Each foot stomp was the beat of the buffalo's hooves. Each swing of the arm was the wind created by the buffalo's stampede. It was joyous and triumphant.

I threw off my shawl and joined.

I had never been a skilled dancer, but that night I felt as graceful as Cousin. I could hear the drum. I could feel it beating in time with my heart as I danced for the many months I had not been allowed to dance. I danced in sadness as I watched my hair being cut and I was given a new name. I danced in understanding as I learned about bridges that would never be built and fear and running away and returning. I danced to my own drum that beat in time to the story I had lived.

Finally both of us stopped, needing no words to know we had each completed our stories. We sat on the steps, trying to catch our breaths. I shivered and wrapped my shawl around my shoulders to keep the chill from seeping into my skin.

"William," I said in Lakota. "Thank you for saving the wotawe Mother made for me. And the wooden rabbit. Thank you for returning them to me."

"My name is not William," he said in Lakota, his black eyes steady.

I waited.

"My tiospaye called me Catches Fire. I received this name when I was three seasons because I tried to catch flames as they danced in the cooking fire." He held up his badly scarred hand. "I learned that you cannot catch flame."

And then he smiled. I had never seen him smile. His whole face changed, becoming open and friendly instead of sullen and closed. I smiled back.

"My name," I answered, "is Four Winds. I earned this name from Uncle when Mother discovered I can understand voices speaking in the trees."

He smiled.

"My sister was named Laughing Wind because when the

winds blew and the rain fell, she loved to stand outside and catch the drops," he said.

"Did you lose your sister?" I asked. He was speaking of her in the past.

"I lost everyone in my tiospaye," he said, looking away from me.

"To illness?" I asked.

"To vengeance," he said. "One night, white soldiers came and set the tipis of my tiospaye on fire. I remember awakening to the smell of smoke and the sounds of screaming and running everywhere.

"I couldn't see and I couldn't tell where Mother and Father were. I crawled away and waited until light came again in the morning."

He was silent for several minutes.

"When I returned, there was nothing left but ashes and aunts and uncles lying dead. I remember calling for Mother and Father and Sister over and over again, but no one answered. So I just began walking. I wandered for a long time, filled with so much fear and grief that I couldn't even remember why I had started walking."

I blinked away tears, thinking about Bear and imagining him wandering lost and confused.

"How old were you?" I asked.

"In the white man's calendar, I believe this happened three years ago. I was almost nine seasons.

"And one day," he continued, "one of the teachers from this school found me wandering, and ill. I had never seen a white woman before, and I thought she was a trickster spirit. I tried to run, but I was too weak. She carried me to this school and took care of me.

"For a long time I could not speak. I could not understand the white man's language. I could not understand this 'William' they kept calling me. I didn't understand why they cut my hair without the mourning wails. I was so confused and so afraid.

"When I finally did try to speak in Lakota, I was beaten. So I learned not to speak, just listen and learn. By then, everyone thought I was slow, and I realized it was better to let them think this."

"Why?" I asked.

"Father once told me that a warrior never lets his enemies see him because then they can hurt him. And at this school I have learned that your spirit can be hurt by your enemies too."

I nodded, understanding.

"You have been as brave as a mighty warrior," I said.

"I have survived," he said.

And then we both sat together in the freezing cold, each of us alone with our thoughts.

SIXTEEN
WINTER COUNT

After that night, something changed within me. I had found a friend, a brother, someone who had learned to keep his spirit alive. I was still trapped at the school. But finding this friend helped calm my angry fire a little.

Cold and snow continued to grip the earth. It had been cold on the reservation too, but our tipis had always felt warm. Their smallness helped trap the heat. At the school there were too many large spaces to keep everything warm. The stove in the schoolroom never got hot enough to heat the whole room. Our sleeping room was always drafty.

In our tiospaye, it was a short walk if we needed to go to another tipi. But at the school, the distance between buildings was long, and the wind would wrap its fingers around our ankles and feet as we walked. Even though I wore leggings beneath my skirts, I was always cold.

Some days the winter winds shook the school in gusts, as if trying to tell us they were angry or unsettled about something we couldn't see.

On those days, Miss Beatrice would bake extra cookies, as if to sweeten the wind to silence.

"It is His way of reminding us of His glory," she would say, thinking we were frightened by the winds. And she would offer her cookies during lessons.

I had never been afraid of the winds. I had grown up in the forests of He Sapa, listening to my ancestors speak through them. That was the true speaking of the winds, not this angry howling that rattled our walls.

"A good strong wind tells us Christmas will be joyous!" Miss Beatrice said. "We have so much to look forward to, children! Now back to lessons. Ignore the winds."

"What's Christmas?" I asked Walks Tall. I had heard the word several times.

"A white holiday," she whispered back.

✵ ✵ ✵

"Tell me more of Christmas," I said to Walks Tall that night as we lay listening to the rattle of the winds.

"It is an important white custom," Moon Awake said. She wrapped herself in her blanket and came to sit near me. Soon others joined us in a huddled circle of blankets.

"They have given us candy sometimes," Walks Tall said.

"Candy?" I asked. "What is that?"

"It is a sweet. It is hard and you can crunch it or you can keep it in your mouth for a long time and it slowly disappears."

"It's delicious," Small Rose said, smacking her lips.

"But they always make sure to tell us that this tradition is not really about candy," Moon Awake added.

"Christmas is when Jesus"—Walks Tall pointed to the tortured man on the wall—"was born."

"They celebrate this?" I asked. "But I thought they killed him. Why would they celebrate his birth?"

I didn't think I would ever understand the white religion, the God, and the Jesus person.

"They celebrate his birth because their god is his father. He is the Son of God," someone said.

"Oh," I said, understanding a little. "I thought the Jesus was the sun in the sky. But he is the *son* and their god is his father. I see why he is important. But I still don't understand why they killed him."

"Miss Margaret said it was part of God's plan."

"I don't understand their god and his plan," I said. "There are so many white customs I don't understand."

The other girls nodded in agreement.

The wind shook the walls, stealing our attention momentarily. For some reason it reminded me of the Winter Counts, our own custom of counting the past year during the season of snow.

No matter how many times I had seen our tiospaye's Winter Count, it still took my breath away. Each winter Uncle would unroll the buffalo hide, and I would stare in awe. Spread out before me was the history of our tiospaye for generations, represented by one symbol for each year.

Uncle was our tiospaye's Keeper. He and the other elders would meet and decide what he should paint on the huge buffalo hide. It was the Keeper's job to add the past season's drawing to the Winter Count.

What would this year's image be? Were they thinking about it right now, at this very moment, as I sat huddled with other girls in the dark? Would the image include my journey to this school?

I threw off my covers and stepped into the cold of the room. I wanted to draw a picture myself, to record my history the way my tiospaye always had.

"If I were to record this past year on the Winter Count," I announced loudly, "it would be the year of Great Change."

No one moved. Moon Awake looked a little frightened, as if she were unsure of what I was going to do next. I was a girl and a child. Girls and children did not draw pictures for the Winter Count. But I yearned to have a familiar custom, something that I knew and understood.

I went to the small wooden chest on the floor where school supplies were kept and found a piece of cloth that Pinch Finger had given us for sewing practice. I dug in another basket for a charcoal pencil and laid the cloth on the floor. In the very center, I drew a picture of a girl. She was weeping, but her hands were held up in a gesture of hope.

"There," I said, holding the cloth up to show the girls. "I have recorded my history for this past year. I have created a Winter Count."

No one moved.

Then Walks Tall stood and took the charcoal pencil from my hand.

"It has been the year of New People," she said, putting the cloth on the floor and drawing a picture next to mine. It showed many girls surrounding one girl, who I knew was me.

"It was the year of cutting hair," another girl said, stepping to the fabric and drawing her own picture of a girl with tears falling down her face alongside strands of hair.

One by one each girl came to the cloth and added her own picture to the unusual Winter Count we had created.

After the last person finished, I rolled the cloth carefully and placed it far beneath my sleeping space so the teachers wouldn't see it.

Everyone was quiet as we climbed back into bed. Even the wind outside had stopped rattling the walls. I felt calm and at peace, happy that we had created our own custom in this place of constant strangeness.

SEVENTEEN
COUNTING COUP

As the days continued, the white holiday Christmas seemed to be the only thing the teachers talked about.

"Christmas is a joyous season," Miss Margaret said during prayers before breakfast. "We enter this season to celebrate the time Christ was born."

Even though I didn't understand the holiday, there was so much happy spirit feeling in the air that I allowed myself to catch it too.

"There is a pine tree with candles on it," Walks Tall said at lunch.

I felt my heart stir at the thought of a pine tree. It had been so long since I had seen one.

"Where is it?" I asked. "I haven't seen pine trees near here. And how do they keep the wind from blowing out the candles?"

"The tree isn't outside. They cut one down and bring it inside," she explained.

"Oh," I said, sad to think of killing a living tree. What a strange custom.

"And gifts. We receive a gift," Moon Awake said.

"Gifts?" I asked.

"It is part of the tradition," Walks Tall explained. "On their Christmas, they exchange gifts. Last year Miss Beatrice gave us mittens that she had knitted."

As if she had read our thoughts, Miss Beatrice announced that our afternoon lesson would be about gift giving and the importance of being selfless.

"We want you each to have a chance to give your family a Christmas gift . . . ," she began.

The word *family* brought a sudden aching thought of Bear. Was he warm and safe or cold and shivering? Was he hungry? Was my tiospaye still getting rations?

"So this afternoon, we have a special guest teacher," she continued. "Miss Agnes."

It was all I could do to keep from groaning out loud

as Pinch Finger stepped to the front, holding small pieces of yarn in her hands.

"Today you will be making a Christmas gift," she said. "When you are finished, it will look like this." She held up a small woven cross.

"This is how you begin . . ." And she talked at us for many minutes, showing the best way to weave our yarn together to make a cross that looked like hers.

I made it look as though I were paying attention.

". . . and then you take it like this," she continued. "And now it is finished. Isn't this lovely?" She held it up for us to see. "You will have something to give your family the next time you see them in the summer. You can use these to help explain the Christian way of life."

I took the yarn Pinch Finger handed me and began weaving. She walked around the room, reviewing our work.

"Yes, Ruth, that is correct. Oh, you need to make it tighter, Anna."

I didn't think I could listen to her talking or pretend I cared about the weaving much longer. I needed to move, to get away from her.

"It's so cold," I said as she came near me. "May I get more wood for the fire?"

"That's William's job," Pinch Finger said, frowning. "Where is that boy?"

No one answered; everyone was intent on their weaving.

"Yes, yes, go, Sarah," Pinch Finger said. "The chill is hard to keep away these days."

As soon as I stepped out into the cold, I felt better.

I listened to the crunching of my feet on the snow as I walked toward the barn. Father had taught me how to tell the temperature by the sound of the snow. The crisper the sound, the colder it was. The snow sounded as if it were cracking with each step, and I could tell it was a very cold day.

Smoke curled from the small chimney of the barn and I thought of the first time I had seen Catches Fire dance. Was he dancing now? Was he ignoring his chores by pretending to be slow?

Cautiously, I cracked one of the large wooden doors and peeked in.

"Catches Fire?" I called quietly in Lakota. Inside it was dark and smelled of wood. It felt warmer than I would have thought, warmer than our schoolroom.

"Four Winds," he answered from the darkness, appearing with a smile on his face.

As my eyes adjusted to the dark I could see piles of wood stacked along the walls, sheltering the barn from the bitter winds. Even with the wood, the walls were painted in streaks of frost. A small stove crackled in the middle of the barn, throwing out heat. Sleeping skins lay nearby on the floor. I realized it looked more like a tipi than my sleeping room, and I felt something catch in my throat.

"You've made a tipi," I said, blinking back tears.

"No one ever comes in here, so no one knows what it looks like or what I've done. And they wouldn't care if they did know. I'm slow, remember?" he said, and I smiled.

Along the beams near his sleeping space I could see carved symbols and pictures.

"Those help to keep the bad dreams away," Catches Fire said, following my gaze.

I walked beneath one beam, following the symbols to a smaller room away from the open space of the barn. A large piece of wood hung in the middle of the room. There were counting marks on it.

"What are these?" I asked. "What are you counting?"

"I am counting coup," he answered proudly.

"Counting coup?" I asked. "How? There are no enemies here. There is no way to count coup."

141

I had spent my childhood hearing stories of men counting coup. It was the supreme act of bravery to touch an enemy in battle without killing him.

"Oh, but there is," he said. "Do you remember when I first came here, I learned it was better not to speak, just to listen and let everyone think I'm slow?" he asked.

I nodded.

"I learned my slowness could interfere with their plans. Every time I stumble. Every time I ruin something for them or cause a delay, it is my way of touching my enemy. And they don't even know I touched them."

I thought of the times I had seen him act slow or clumsy and realized it usually caused a problem for a teacher. He would stumble while carrying wood for a fire, delaying the start of the fire. He would slip and drop a basket of pencils so that one of the teachers would have to scurry to collect them before they rolled beneath the floorboards. He would act dazed and confused when asked a question during lessons. Not only had he learned to use his slowness as protection, he had learned to use it as a weapon.

I smiled. He grinned back at me.

"This is where I keep count." He pointed to the piece of wood. "This is where I look to remember that I have my own way of counting coup. I have my own way of showing bravery."

"There are dozens of marks," I murmured.

"There is something else," he said, walking to a corner and taking several pieces of wood from the top of burlap. Beneath the burlap was a large flour sack. Carefully, he reached into the sack and pulled out a small doll.

"This belongs to Moon Awake," he said.

He reached in again and pulled out a small star shape sewn on a piece of quilt. "Walks Tall's," he announced.

"Are these?" I whispered.

He nodded.

"My instructions were to burn them," he said. "At one time this sack held a small wooden rabbit and a wotawe."

"Good-luck pieces," I whispered, amazed by what he had done.

He nodded. "They were tossed in with the clothing, and I was ordered to burn them. But I couldn't. They are too important. And some day, I will return them to their owners."

He put everything back, covering the sack with the burlap and pieces of wood again.

Suddenly I had an idea.

"Catches Fire," I said, feeling excitement grow. "This Christmas everyone keeps talking about. It is a time of giving gifts."

"Yes," he said. "It is."

"The good-luck pieces," I said. "Perhaps this Christmas is the time for their return?"

A smile appeared on his face, and I knew he understood what I was thinking.

"William!"

The harsh call of Pastor Huber in the doorway made me jump.

"What are you doing, William?" Pastor Huber screamed. "Who are you talking to?"

I walked quickly to the door.

"I needed wood, Pastor Huber," I said, trembling.

The pastor kept the door open with one foot so that he was still standing outside. He blew on his hands, rubbing them together for warmth.

"William!" Pastor Huber yelled. "It is wrong for you to have a girl in here. You know this!"

Catches Fire walked over to us slowly, handing me a small piece of wood.

"Of course he doesn't know this," Pastor Huber mumbled

to himself as he pulled me out the door. "Stupid savage."

I winced.

Catches Fire brought another piece of wood that was even smaller than the first.

"Well, don't just give her one piece at a time!" Pastor Huber shouted, and Catches Fire ambled over slowly and gathered two more logs, almost dropping one, then placing them in my arms.

His whole body had changed. He had become "slow."

"Get the wood and get back to the schoolroom!" Pastor Huber barked at me.

I turned toward the school but glanced back to see if Catches Fire would be punished. He had a look on his face I recognized. His eyes were vacant, as if he were staring at something no one else could see. Pastor Huber had already left the barn and was grumbling to himself. I smiled, knowing Catches Fire would add another mark to his count.

"Sarah, at last!" Pinch Finger snapped when I returned. "What took you so long? We're almost out of wood, and it is so cold outside!"

She took the wood from my arms, and I sat back down at my bench. The other girls had finished their crosses and were wrapping them in small squares of burlap.

"Why are you tying them inside burlap?" I asked Moon Awake. "Are you hiding them?"

"No. The whites wrap their gifts before they give them to each other."

"Now let's sing a Christmas carol!" Miss Beatrice said, and she began to sing. "Silent night, holy night. All is calm. All is bright."

I finished my cross but didn't join in the singing with the others. My mind was too full of thoughts of counting coup and too excited by the thought of the things Catches Fire had hidden in the barn.

✶ ✶ ✶

After evening meal, Miss Beatrice called me into the kitchen.

"Please come with me, Sarah," she said. "I am making Christmas cookies, and I need your help."

"Yes, Miss Beatrice," I said, following her.

The cooking room was full of things I had never seen before. Large pans hung from hooks and a huge oven stood against a wall. There was even a sink, something I hadn't known existed before coming to the school. This sink could hold several pots of heated water for washing dishes.

A lump of cookie batter sat on a table. Miss Beatrice took a rolling pin and began to flatten the dough.

"I'll roll the dough, and you can cut it into cookies," she said, handing me a small knife.

As we worked, Miss Beatrice hummed.

"Things seem better, Sarah," she said.

"What do you mean, Miss Beatrice?" I asked, confused.

"You seem less angry. Happier to be here. I'm glad for this. I'm glad you came back."

"But I didn't come back. I was brought back."

"Oh, there is always a choice," Miss Beatrice said. "Sometimes it can be hard to understand God's will."

I nodded, but I didn't know what my return had to do with her god's will.

"You are an interesting student," she continued. "Different from those I've known before. You are . . ." She stopped, as if struggling to find the right word. "More independent. Free, perhaps. The other girls look up to you."

I looked at her, surprised.

"They see you as a kind of leader. They pay attention to what you do. This is a gift, this leadership. When you ran from us, the other girls were devastated. They were so happy to hear you were coming back. And I was too. I enjoy being your teacher."

"Oh," I said, looking up at her. "I . . . well . . . Thank you."

I had never thought about leaders. Leaders were the elders, not the children. Was it possible for someone to lead if they weren't an elder?

EIGHTEEN
GIFTS

Over the next few days, Catches Fire brought me the good-luck pieces he had saved, one at a time. With the cold it was easy to hide them beneath shawls.

I carried them carefully to my sleeping space and tucked them inside small holes I had made in my pillow and winter quilt.

I began to join Catches Fire at the lunch meal break.

"May I eat with you?" I had asked the first time I joined him.

The entire room had grown silent. Everyone had stopped eating. I looked over to see Walks Tall and Moon Awake staring at me.

He nodded, and I sat down next to him. We ate without talking, and I noticed that no one else in the room was talking either. Most of the girls were watching me and Catches Fire.

Miss Beatrice looked up from her desk where she had been eating.

"My goodness. It has become so quiet." Then she saw me with Catches Fire. "I see there are new friendships being made."

"Yes, Miss Beatrice," I said, and smiled at Catches Fire.

Slowly, the other girls went back to eating and the room filled with the sound of talking again.

After our lunch that day I stayed next to Catches Fire during the lessons that followed. Even though it wasn't my assigned place to sit, Miss Beatrice let me stay. While reading, I could see that he was struggling with some of the words in his reading book.

"This is the word *capture*, do you see?" I leaned over and whispered.

He nodded, smiling slightly. I felt happy to know I could help him in a small way after he had helped me so much.

❊ ❊ ❊

The next day Catches Fire brought me Moon Awake's small doll, whispering, "This is the last," as he slipped it into my hand.

I nodded, smiling. I would give the gifts to the girls that night at bedtime.

I could barely sit still during our evening meal. Bedtime prayers seemed to drag on forever. But finally Miss Margaret finished.

"Blessings to you, girls," Miss Margaret said after we had finished prayers and then crawled beneath thick quilts, trying to get warm in the frigid night air.

"And to you," we repeated, saying the words we always said when Miss Margaret led prayers.

Someone blew out the lanterns and the room fell dark.

"The white Christmas is in a few days," I said quietly.

"Go to sleep, Four Winds," someone whispered. "It's too cold to talk tonight."

Another girl murmured agreement.

"But who can sleep when there are gifts to give?" I said.

"What do you mean?" Moon Awake asked, suddenly interested.

I reached inside my quilt and searched for the small doll I knew belonged to her.

"This," I said, going to her and placing the doll in her hand, "is your present of Christmas."

She gasped as she realized what it was. "How? How did you get this?" she asked. "I . . . I thought it was lost. Favorite Aunt made it for me."

Suddenly the other girls were out of their beds, gathering around Moon Awake.

"Yours," I said, bringing out a tiny carved flower and handing it to Small Rose.

She took it with a delighted gasp.

I continued giving back objects the girls had brought with them from their homes: a felted buffalo, a sewn fabric star, a tiny doll, a piece of beaded hide. All things they thought were gone forever.

"I didn't think I would ever see this again," Walks Tall said tearfully as she clutched a small piece of quilt.

"How did you get these things?" Small Rose asked.

"It was Catches Fire," I said. "William. He was supposed to burn them, but he saved them. He has kept them safe."

Stunned silence filled the room.

"The boy William?" Moon Awake asked in disbelief. "The boy William did this?"

"But he's slow," Walks Tall said.

"No," I said, "he's brave and he's smart."

Moon Awake looked at her doll. "And his name is Catches Fire?" she asked.

"Yes," I answered.

"He is the keeper of things lost," Walks Tall said.

"And now they are found," I said, nodding.

We stood looking at each other in the moonlight and then someone started to dance. Spontaneously everyone joined. We stepped quietly, carefully, so that no one below would hear. It was silent, but it was joyful. This dance and our treasures belonged to us.

NINETEEN
LAUGHING DEER

Then unexpectedly, only days before the white holiday, an empty sleeping space appeared next to mine.

"Another girl is coming to us," the girls whispered.

The room buzzed with excitement. Who would this new girl be? Where was she coming from? Why was she here?

When the new girl arrived the next evening, small and fragile, she reminded me of how frightened I had been when I first came to the school.

She stood trembling in the middle of the room where Pinch Finger had left her. This new girl was young, perhaps only a few seasons older than Bear. She was much younger than the rest of us.

My heart ached as I stared at her long black hair, knowing it would be cut soon. It was rich and full and hung down to the middle of her back. I had almost forgotten how long and beautiful hair was supposed to be.

I studied her clothes. Her winter shawl had already been removed, and I thought of Catches Fire, who would probably be burning it at that moment.

"Come," I whispered to her in Lakota, "next to me."

She grabbed me, sobbing, Lakota words pouring from her.

"Who are you?" she asked. "Are you Lakota? Are you white?"

"I am Four Winds," I said quietly. "And this is Walks Tall and Moon Awake."

"I am Laughing Deer." She hiccupped between sobs.

I stared at her. Laughing Deer had been Cousin's name.

"You must not use this name anyplace but in this room," Walks Tall continued, stepping close and bending down to the little girl.

I remembered hearing the same words when I first arrived.

"You will get a white name and you will have to use it," Walks Tall said, helping the small child into her night-clothes. "But in this room we will call you Laughing Deer."

The other girls stayed away. They dressed in nightclothes silently, watching the new child try to piece together what was happening.

"Do you have anything from your tiospaye?" Moon Awake whispered.

Laughing Deer nodded, pulling a small piece of sandstone from her pocket. It had been carved into the shape of a circle.

Gently, I took the stone from her hand.

"No, no!" she cried, grabbing for it. "Father gave it to me! I am supposed to keep it with me. It will protect me!"

"I will keep it safe," I said, showing her the small hole in my pillow where I tucked it in carefully. "It must be hidden, or they will take it."

✿ ✿ ✿

The next morning Laughing Deer disappeared after breakfast and reappeared later in the schoolroom, tears frozen on her face. Her hair had been trimmed and tied into two small braids. Pinch Finger dragged her into the room, then stood watching.

Laughing Deer huddled in the back of the room. When

she saw me, she darted over and nestled between me and Catches Fire.

"Well, that is really not where you are supposed to sit," Miss Beatrice started to say, and then stopped. "But I suppose for now I will allow it."

Laughing Deer climbed onto my lap, and even though this was not proper school behavior, Miss Beatrice said nothing.

I stroked her hair, trying to comfort her, knowing how confused and frightened she felt.

"Mary," Miss Beatrice announced to everyone, pointing to Laughing Deer, who looked completely bewildered.

"Mary," we all repeated.

"This is your new white name," I whispered softly in Lakota when Miss Beatrice turned back to the front. "This is what we will call you everywhere except in our sleeping room. My white name is Sarah. And hers is Anna." I pointed to Walks Tall, who sat a few rows away.

"I don't understand," she said in Lakota.

No one moved except Pinch Finger, who was at Laughing Deer's side immediately.

"No!" she said, pinching Laughing Deer's ear hard. "You do not speak those savage words! No, Mary!"

Tears welled in Laughing Deer's eyes. I put my finger to my lips and shook my head.

✧ ✧ ✧

Over the next few days, Laughing Deer stayed close by me. I did all that I could to protect her from being hit.

"You do not just call out when you have something to say," I told her on her second school day. "You must stand and wait for the teacher to come to you or say your name."

She nodded.

"And remember, your name in this room is Mary. That is what everyone will call you. But also remember that your real name is Laughing Deer. Don't forget that."

"I won't," she said.

Miss Beatrice let Laughing Deer stay near me, and I helped her with lessons, teaching her about the stick marks called letters and how letters turned into words.

She was a quick learner, and her spirit reminded me of Bear. She was curious about everything and excited when she mastered several small words.

I wondered how Bear would react if he were sent to this school. He was bursting with constant excitement and full of curiosity. But when he didn't understand the reason for things, he was also stubborn. How would he survive at the school when so many things didn't make sense? How would he survive in the white world?

At night Laughing Deer would take out the small rock from my pillow and hold it tightly. Sometimes she would cry as she lay in her sleeping space. Moon Awake would rub her arm or I would stroke her hair, knowing we couldn't take away her loneliness but hoping we could somehow ease it.

Sometimes I would lie awake and watch her sleep in the space next to mine. Other times I would go to the window and scrape the frost away and look down, longing to see Catches Fire in his dance. Many times I felt like crying myself, knowing the way the teachers would work to remove the Indian from this young girl.

TWENTY
CHRISTMAS

The day of Christmas arrived with fresh new snow. Instead of school lessons, we spent the morning in the church service with Pastor Huber.

"His birth brought us hope. He is the light in the darkness," he said, wearing his usual fierce expression.

All of the teachers sat in the front row, watching Pastor Huber with expressions of admiration, as if the words coming from his mouth were full of wisdom. They nodded as he spoke.

"He saved all of mankind with His coming," he continued.

I looked outside to see snow falling in light, fluffy flakes. It made me think of my family. For them, this white holiday was just another day of trying to keep warm, of trying to find enough to eat. I pictured each of them—Bear, Mother, Father, and Uncle—hoping they were safe and warm. Tears welled in my eyes, thinking about how much I missed them.

"Yes!" Pastor Huber exclaimed, walking toward me. "Do you see? Sarah has an understanding of the importance of this day. Do you see her tears?"

I straightened, wiping my eyes, embarrassed that everyone was looking at me.

After the church service, we gathered to play games outside in the snow.

"Snow angels!" Moon Awake called, dropping to the ground.

Everyone formed a circle to create snow angels with interlocking wings.

Soft giggles floated in the air, and I looked over to see Laughing Deer. It was the first time I had seen her smile, the first time she had ventured from my side. Her laughter was musical. It sounded much like Cousin's.

"Look," I whispered to her in Lakota when she came running to me, smiling and out of breath. "Look at the circle. They call them angels, but it looks like a tiospaye dancing."

She nodded and then raced off to gather snow into a small ball that she could throw at someone.

❊ ❊ ❊

The evening meal was a feast. It was filled with foods I had never seen, ham and pies and spiced apples and potatoes that had been mashed into a creamy mixture. Twists of colored sweets lay on our plates.

"There's candy to help celebrate Christmas," Pinch Finger announced with a smile.

I leaned over to Laughing Deer, whose eyes had widened at the sight of all the food.

"Be careful," I whispered. "Don't eat too much or you will be sick. Take small bites."

She nodded, but I could tell it would be hard for her not to eat as much as she could.

"And for this special occasion, Brother Huber is joining us," Pinch Finger said as the other teachers brought out bowls of steaming food.

The pastor seated himself. "Let us pray . . . ," he began. Everyone bowed their heads, listening to his prayer of thanks.

I peeked through my closed hands, wondering about

Catches Fire, hoping that he was warm in the barn. He had not been invited to join us for this meal.

"And now, we eat," Pastor Huber said. Something that almost looked like a smile crossed his lips.

There was laughter and talking and we ate until the food was gone. It was festive and joyful, and even Pastor Huber laughed at something that someone said.

Laughing Deer giggled even though I knew she didn't understand why she was laughing.

"I am proud of you," I said. "You show much strength." She had been careful while eating, taking only small bites of the strange foods.

She smiled back at me, her eyes shining.

When we had finished the meal, I put one end of a candy twist in my mouth, enjoying the unusual sweet taste.

"Now, let's gather," Pinch Finger announced after we had cleared the table and cleaned the dishes. "In the parlor!" she said, leading us to the sitting room.

I had never spent time in this room, and I noticed that a fire burned inside the small wall space in the corner. Large puffy chairs made of patterned fabric with matching pillows were in the room. A pine tree that had tiny lit candles on it stood in another corner. My nose was hit with the smell of pine, and I closed my eyes momentarily, filled with the memory of a rich forest.

"Is this the tradition of Christmas you told me of?" I asked Moon Awake, pointing at the tree.

She nodded.

"It makes me think of He Sapa," I said.

Moon Awake nodded. "Me too."

"But it also makes me sad. Where did they find this tree? I haven't seen any pine trees here. And why did they kill this living thing? I don't understand."

"There are many strange customs during this season," Moon Awake answered.

"Quiet, children. Settle yourselves," Pinch Finger said, directing us to sit on the floor or in the chairs. Once everyone was seated, she went to the tree and pulled out a long roll of burlap from beneath it.

"Do you remember this, girls?" she asked.

I felt a small shiver as I recognized the banner. The last time I had seen it, it only had words penciled in. But since then, the girls had finished their work. It now read ALL SAINTS MISSIONARY SCHOOL in different colors of thread. I shivered at the memory of being sent to get scissors and then being beaten.

"This is your Christmas gift this year," Pinch Finger continued. "Mr. Merton, from town, has generously donated his services to take our photograph with the banner you decorated. It will be the first photograph in our school's history."

Almost timidly, Miss Beatrice stepped forward. "And I knitted you something too," she said. "Scarves to keep out the cold."

"Yes, yes," Pinch Finger cut in. "The scarves are nice. But your real gift is the photograph. Mr. Merton will be here tomorrow to take it right here in our parlor, in front of the Christmas tree!"

Laughing Deer looked up at me, smiling, unable to understand what had been said but noticing that it made Pinch Finger happy. I smiled back so she wouldn't be frightened. But images of the plaque ran through my mind. Kill the Indian, save the man.

✵ ✵ ✵

That night there was much talk of this photograph.

"I saw a photograph once," Small Rose said. "It looked like a drawing but it was a perfect drawing."

"What makes the drawing?" I asked.

"A spirit box," Small Rose answered. "It captures your spirit forever."

I didn't like the idea of my spirit being captured. Was this another part of the white god I didn't understand?

As Miss Beatrice finished prayers in our sleeping room that night, I wanted to ask her about the photograph.

"Miss Beatrice?" I asked when she came to me.

"Yes?" she said.

"I . . . I want . . . ," I began, but realized there were many things I wanted to ask. I wanted to know about the spirit box, but I also wanted to know about Christmas, about wrapping gifts, and about a god who loves and punishes at the same time. And why this god loves the whites but hates the Indians.

But all that came out was, "I want to thank you for the scarf."

"You are very welcome," she said, her face brightening. She leaned over and kissed my forehead. "And a merry Christmas to you," she said. Then she added, "I am happy you are here with us." Then she blew out the lanterns and left the room.

TWENTY-ONE
SPIRIT BOX

The next day we were directed into the parlor after the morning meal. A white man waited inside the room next to a small box perched high on top of three wooden legs.

"That's the spirit box," Small Rose whispered as we filed in. "That's what will capture our spirits for the photograph."

I studied the box. It was smaller than I had imagined.

"Over here, girls. Sit down," Pinch Finger directed happily.

She pulled girls in and out of places, seating someone here, moving another girl there. Finally we were all sitting near the Christmas tree. Miss Margaret lit the candles on the branches so that the tree glowed softly.

"William," Pinch Finger called in a loud, slow voice. "It is time. You may join us."

Catches Fire ambled from the kitchen area. I was happy to see him. The photograph would not have felt complete without him.

Pinch Finger grabbed him by the arm and pulled him to a place in the back where he was almost hidden.

"Now take this banner," she said, giving one end to Walks Tall, "and you take the other end," she said to Laughing Deer, who had to hold it up to her chin so that it was level.

"We are ready, Mr. Merton," she said. "Girls, stand still. Look straight ahead at the camera. Do not move."

"Okay, children," Mr. Merton said in a deep voice. "You mustn't move at all." He crawled beneath a blanket near the spirit box and counted. "One. Two. Three!"

There was a bright flash of light and a puff of smoke, and for an instant I could see nothing except huge spots floating in front of my eyes.

I had expected something more than a single flash of light. But Mr. Merton gathered his spirit box, and Miss Margaret hurried us to lessons in the schoolroom. I was disappointed by how quickly the entire photograph had taken place. I had thought there would be a ceremony of some kind.

✵ ✵ ✵

After that, the winter season settled in with cold that bit our ankles and fingers and threatened to dampen our spirits. The excitement of Christmas had gone, leaving behind the boring routine of lessons and short, cold days.

Being unable to go outside made the school days feel even longer, and I looked forward to our small breaks for meals, even though they had to be inside.

The other girls had slowly come to join me and Catches Fire for lunch meals. One by one, they joined us as we sat and ate lunch together. Eventually, we all became one circle around the stove during meal breaks. Miss Beatrice sat at her table at the front of the schoolroom and ate her lunch, pretending not to hear if we spoke in Lakota.

Sometimes Laughing Deer would crawl into someone's lap for a story. Other times Catches Fire would show us a new game.

"There is a game we used to play," he said one especially gloomy day. "A hunting game. These are my sticks," he said, gathering four slate pencils.

He sat down on the floor and arranged them carefully in front of him. "You must guess the number I have just made using my sticks. But remember, this is a hunting game, so the number will be hidden."

"This is too easy," Moon Awake said. "There are four sticks. So the number is four."

Catches Fire shook his head, a glimmer in his eye.

Moon Awake frowned.

"Try this," Catches Fire said, rearranging the four sticks into a different pattern.

"But it's still four," Moon Awake said.

"No," Catches Fire said, grinning. "The number is two."

He leaned over and whispered something to Laughing Deer, who clapped her hands together with delight.

"But how can it be two when there are still four sticks there?" Moon Awake argued.

"Remember, this is a hunting game," he replied, scooping up the sticks and dropping them in a random pile. "You have to look for things that aren't easy to see."

"Me now!" Laughing Deer said, using white words that she was starting to remember.

"Yes," Catches Fire agreed. "You try." And he took one of the sticks away and arranged the other three in a long line.

Laughing Deer stood up and walked around Catches Fire, examining the sticks from different directions, trying to add to the suspense.

Then she sat down and said, "Number eight."

"Correct!" Catches Fire said, and there were groans from the other girls.

I looked up to see Miss Beatrice standing nearby, watching.

"You do it now," Catches Fire said, handing Laughing Deer the three sticks.

She carefully arranged them, then sat so they were in front of her.

"This is a hunting game," Catches Fire repeated. "Hunters must notice things that are not always easy to see." He nodded, gesturing for us to look at Laughing Deer more carefully.

Walks Tall was the first to see. "Oh," she cried, "it's the number seven!"

"Yes," Laughing Deer said, and giggled.

And then I saw what Walks Tall had seen. Laughing Deer was holding out seven fingers. I laughed out loud. It was so clear. We had all been looking so carefully at the sticks, that we hadn't even noticed her fingers. The sticks had nothing to do with the number. Her fingers had everything to do with it.

"Enough!" Pinch Finger had come into the schoolroom.

We all jumped, and Laughing Deer picked up the sticks quickly.

"Enough of these silly games," Pinch Finger said. "William, your help is needed in the church."

Catches Fire stood and got his cloak and ambled slowly out of the room. A few girls giggled to see him acting as if he didn't understand.

"And what is so funny?" Pinch Finger asked. Behind her were two men I had never seen before. They wore shiny pointed shoes and pants with small stripes on them. One of them had a tall hat on his head. Their expressions were stern.

"Children, return to your seats," she said. "Miss Beatrice, these are the senators I told you about."

Miss Beatrice smiled and curtsied. "It is lovely to meet you. I am so happy you were able to come to our school and see what we do here."

I watched with curiosity. What were senators? And why were they at this school?

"This is certainly one of our biggest success stories,"

Pinch Finger was saying. She gently pulled Laughing Deer up out of her seat.

"This is Mary and she has not been with us long. She mastered English quickly." Pinch Finger stood with her arms on Laughing Deer's shoulders. Laughing Deer blushed.

"When she was able to speak English, she spoke in complete sentences. I think it is a true testament to the ways we are trying to civilize these people."

Civilize these people. *Kill the Indian, save the man.* I clenched my fists to help hold my anger inside.

"Show these nice men how you say your prayers, Mary," Pinch Finger prodded.

Laughing Deer put her hands together and bowed her head, repeating the meal prayer we said. I knew she didn't understand the words. She had asked me to explain this ritual, and I could not because I did not understand it myself.

The men clapped their hands together.

"And there are other things I want to show you," Pinch Finger continued, dismissing Laughing Deer back to her seat. "We are going to bring her to the town fair and show everyone what she can do. She will be our own little ambassador."

She continued talking to the men as she led them out of the schoolroom. Miss Beatrice turned back to our arithmetic lesson, and I bent over my slate as if I were paying attention.

But all I could think about was how young Laughing Deer was and how close in age she was to Bear. Bear wouldn't understand this white world any more than she did. But he would do anything for food. He would repeat prayers he didn't understand. He would perform for the teachers and blush with pride at their praise. He would lose himself just as I feared Laughing Deer might lose herself.

TWENTY-TWO
REALIZATION

After dinner a few days later, Miss Margaret gathered us again in the sitting room. Miss Beatrice and Pinch Finger were already there.

"It has arrived, girls!" Pinch Finger said so cheerfully that it almost sounded like a song.

"What? What arrived?" Laughing Deer asked, bouncing on the balls of her feet.

"The photograph. Mr. Merton delivered it this morning, but I wanted to save it until after evening meal and prayers. I knew that once you saw it you would be so excited you wouldn't be able to concentrate on your studies." She walked over to a small table and lifted a large cloth-covered rectangle.

"We will hang it right here in this room," she said.

Dramatically, she removed the cloth.

"Step closely so you can see," she encouraged. "Isn't it beautiful?"

I peeked around someone's arm to see the most perfect drawing I had ever seen. It was clear and crisp and showed the exact details of the inside of the parlor.

"Do you remember when this photograph was taken?" the teacher asked. "You worked so hard on the banner."

I peered closer and saw that it was not really a drawing. It was an actual image of the room. And in the image were many white girls standing behind a banner that read ALL SAINTS MISSIONARY SCHOOL. All the girls were dressed the same and had neatly trimmed hair in braids.

Slowly, I realized this was the image the spirit box had made. It had not captured our spirits and taken them away as I had feared. Somehow it had put images of children on a large piece of stiff paper.

But the girls in the picture were white girls.

"But who are these people?" I asked.

"Us," Walks Tall answered, pointing to one girl.

"No," I said, shaking my head.

"Look, Mary, that is you." Pinch Finger lifted Laughing

Deer so she could get a better look. "Do you see how wonderful you look? How much you have changed already since you've been with us?"

I looked back and forth from Laughing Deer to the photograph and realized the girl in the photograph was Laughing Deer.

"And that is you," Pinch Finger said to me, touching the face of another girl in the photograph.

I shook my head. That was not me. I could not have mistaken myself for a white girl.

"No," I whispered, trembling.

"Yes, it is you, Sarah," Pinch Finger said. "You look lovely. You all look lovely." She hugged the photograph to herself, then placed it gently on a table. "Now let's sing a hymn!"

The sounds of song floated around me, but I felt trapped, like a rabbit entangled in a snare.

"I . . . ," I said loudly, interrupting the hymn. Pinch Finger stopped.

"What is it?" she asked with irritation.

"I . . ." I wanted to lash out, to hit, to run. I looked at Laughing Deer and thought of Bear. "I want to help make bread," I said in a rush, unable to think of anything else.

"Well, you don't have to interrupt," said Pinch Finger.

"It is not the way a proper lady behaves. Miss Beatrice can always use help in the kitchen." And she pointed in that direction.

I walked to the kitchen with Miss Beatrice.

"Sarah," she said, touching my shoulder.

I pulled away from her hand as if it were hot. I did not want to be touched, and I did not want to talk.

"The dough is ready for kneading," she said, and then she walked out of the kitchen, letting me pound on the dough until my fists ached.

❖ ❖ ❖

I had frightful dreams that night and awoke in the dark. Quietly, I found my winter shawl and crept outside into the cold. I needed to talk to Catches Fire.

Once I reached the barn, I opened the door as carefully as I could, trying to keep it from creaking. The glow from the small stove was the only light I could see inside the darkness.

"Catches Fire?" I whispered.

"Yes," he answered. He stood and beckoned me inside, then went and put another piece of wood in the stove. He sat, and I joined him on the ground.

I sat, clutching my knees, trying to keep warm, trying to find the words to explain how I felt.

"The photograph," I finally blurted out. "Have you seen it?"

He nodded.

"I saw a white girl standing with many other white girls. But they were us. It was me! I thought I was a white girl!"

"Yes," he said quietly.

I began to sob, letting all my anger and sadness pour out.

Catches Fire nudged closer so that our knees touched. He did not speak, just let me cry.

"I am so afraid, Catches Fire," I said. "The buffalo are gone. We live on reservations and we are not allowed to leave. We're starving. The teachers want to kill the Indian. I see Laughing Deer and I think of my little brother and how he would do anything for food. Will they take him too? They have taken everything else!"

"They have taken many things," Catches Fire said quietly. "But they cannot have everything. They cannot see everything."

"What do you mean?" I asked.

"They cannot have our spirit. It is like the hunting game I showed you. Sometimes you can't see everything."

I thought of the way he counted coup, the way he was able to look slow and awkward when really he was smart and graceful.

"But I'm not like you," I said. "I can't do what you have done. I can't hide inside myself and stay protected."

We stayed side by side in front of the stove, saying nothing more. I felt my eyes grow heavy as I watched the flames flicker. Catches Fire nudged me, and I realized I had fallen asleep.

"You must return, Four Winds," he said. "Before the others awaken."

I nodded and found my way back to my sleeping space.

TWENTY-THREE
UNDERSTANDING

Thoughts of the photograph haunted me. It was as if the angry spirit I had been able to keep quiet for so long was loose again, waiting for its chance to be free. I didn't think I could stand one more day at the school. But I couldn't leave, or my family would starve.

I had become like a moth I had once seen tangled in a spider's web. The more the moth struggled, the more entangled it became until the spider came and made the moth its meal.

I was angry and short with everyone.

At our evening meal, Walks Tall tripped and spilled water on my dress.

I lashed out. "How can you be so clumsy?" I screamed at her. "You need to watch where you walk with those big feet!"

I should have felt shame to see the hurt look on Walks Tall's face, but I didn't.

"Come with me, Sarah," Miss Beatrice said, standing. "I need help with the bread."

"No," I said. I heard someone gasp at my disobedience.

"Come . . . with me . . . now," Miss Beatrice said slowly.

I stomped into the kitchen, where several lumps of dough had been left to rise.

"You take that one, and I'll start with this one," she said, pointing.

I took one of the lumps of dough and began pounding.

"I always wanted to be a teacher," Miss Beatrice said.

I focused on beating the dough, ignoring her words.

"Children are so important. Teaching them is so important. And I always wanted to bring them God's word."

As I pounded, I felt my anger leave and sadness come. I missed my family. I wanted to be able to dance and speak my language. But I was trapped. I began to cry.

Miss Beatrice looked at me and then back at her dough.

"Kneading dough can help work out all sorts of things," she said, and spent a few seconds in silence, focused on her hands. "That's the thing about teaching," she continued. "When you teach, you can help a child become something different, perhaps something she didn't even know she could become. It's almost like the child is standing on one side of a riverbank and the teacher is standing on the other side. The teacher creates a bridge for the child to cross."

I stopped pounding and stared at her.

"But," I said, "bridges . . ."

"Yes?" she asked.

"Never mind," I said.

After we had finished and Miss Beatrice had dismissed me, I trudged up to the sleeping room, where the other girls had already said prayers.

Laughing Deer came and took my hand, leading me to my sleeping space.

Walks Tall glanced at me. I was sure she knew I had been crying.

"Join us," she said. "We are telling stories."

"Walks Tall," I said, trying not to cry again. "I'm sorry."

She nodded and pulled me into the circle.

After the stories we crawled into bed and I turned away from the others. I kept thinking about Miss Beatrice and bridges and teachers.

They see you as a kind of leader, she had said before. *They pay attention to what you do.*

I thought of Laughing Deer and how she followed me, listening to and obeying everything I said. She wanted nothing more than to please others. She would do anything the teachers asked, even if she didn't understand it.

I wished I could help Laughing Deer understand the importance of protecting her spirit. I wished I could help her understand more about the Great White Father and the way he broke promises.

I thought again of how much she reminded me of Bear, how he always tried so hard to please the elders. I wished I could help him understand the things I had learned so he could live in this new white world.

I looked out the window in our sleeping space and stared at the stars dotting the sky. I thought of the polestar and the way it had guided me back to my tiospaye when I had run away.

And then I realized there was a way I could help my people. Perhaps I wasn't trapped like a moth in a spider's web. Perhaps I didn't need a bridge at all. I could show my people how to cross the rushing waters another way.

Are you brave? I could hear Cousin whisper in my ear.

I already knew the answer.

TWENTY-FOUR
CHOICE

Before morning meal, I found Catches Fire. He was near the barn, fixing a harness for a horse.

"Do you remember I told you I used to think I was meant to be a bridge for my people?" I asked.

He nodded.

"But I realized this is not a place of building bridges, and I am trapped here."

"Yes," he said, nodding.

"Miss Beatrice spoke with me last night. And later, I had an understanding."

He said nothing, waiting for me to continue.

"This understanding helped me realize I can help my

people. And I am not trapped."

He looked confused.

"I want to teach," I said in a rush, needing to hear the words out loud.

"You want to teach?" he asked. "Why?"

"I don't want to teach here," I explained. "I want to teach my tiospaye. Even if this is not a place of building bridges, I can still help my people. I can teach them the white language and the white numbers. But more important," I said, feeling excited by the idea, "I can teach them the things you cannot see. I can help them understand the white customs and the ways of the white world. I can be my own kind of bridge for my people into the white world.

"Perhaps it is like the hunting game you showed us," I continued. "After being here I understand parts of the white world that others may not be able to see. And perhaps I can use this understanding to help my people."

"Perhaps," he said.

☼ ☼ ☼

During lessons that afternoon I stood and waited for Miss Beatrice to acknowledge me.

"Do you need help with your arithmetic, Sarah?" she asked.

"No, I would like to help you with bread tonight, please," I said.

"Of course," she answered. "Come to the kitchen after evening meal and prayers."

In the cooking room that night we began by kneading dough. I knew what I wanted to say, but was too afraid to start.

"Is there something you wish to tell me, Sarah?" Miss Beatrice asked after we had worked in silence.

"I have been thinking," I said, "about what you told me of teaching."

"I always wanted to be a teacher," she said.

"Yes," I said, taking a deep breath and saying the words before I lost my courage. "I want to be a teacher too."

"Oh, Sarah, that is wonderful!" she said, smiling. "You can certainly help with little Mary. And William seems to be progressing. You work so well with him. I think you have a natural gift. There might even be someone in town who could use your teaching help. Perhaps we could arrange for you to be a tutor."

"No," I said quietly. "I want to teach my people."

She frowned.

"I want to teach my people how to speak English. I want to teach them arithmetic," I continued. *I want to be like the polestar, helping to guide my people through this white world*, I thought but did not say.

She opened her mouth and closed it again.

I thought of the hunting game I had learned from Catches Fire. "Maybe it is God's will," I said in a rush, trying to use her words so that she would understand. "Maybe He is the one who has brought me here so this can happen."

Her face brightened.

"Sarah, I think I understand," she said. "I will talk to Miss Agnes about this and Pastor Huber, of course."

TWENTY-FIVE
SPRING

The birds had begun to talk in the early mornings. The sun stayed longer in the sky, and I knew the earth was ready for a new season. I looked forward to the sight of plants awakening and the changing of the moons.

But this also meant much time had passed since I had spoken with Miss Beatrice about teaching my people. I was afraid she had forgotten our talk. I feared I was not going to be allowed to teach. I was not going to be allowed to return to my tiospaye.

Lessons continued. Prayers were said. Pastor Huber lectured during the church service. Nothing in the white world changed except that it was warmer outside.

Then one day Pinch Finger came to the schoolroom. She had not been there for several weeks, and I thought perhaps she had come to watch Miss Beatrice again. To my surprise, she motioned to me.

She said nothing as she led me through the house and into the parlor. Pastor Huber was there, sitting in one of the chairs. Another white man I had never seen before sat in a chair near him.

There were two other white men in the room who looked familiar. But I wasn't sure where I had seen them before.

I began to tremble, certain I was in trouble.

"Sit, Sarah," Pastor Huber said.

I noticed the school photograph on the wall above the chair where he sat. I shuddered.

"This is Pastor Aken," Pastor Huber said, pointing to the man sitting closest to him. "He oversees our school."

I nodded, thinking he must be someone of importance.

"And you remember the senators who were here several months ago," Pinch Finger said, pointing to the two men.

They were the visitors who had clapped and laughed when Laughing Deer had recited prayers. That was why they looked familiar.

"Miss Agnes has told us you want to teach English,"

Pastor Aken spoke. His voice was quiet and low.

I began to tremble again. But not from fear, from excitement. *Be brave*, I thought to myself, and nodded.

"This has not been done before. It would be highly unusual," Pastor Aken continued.

"Based on our success with some of the other children, it would be logical," Pinch Finger said.

"An experiment worth trying," one of the senators added. "If it is successful, the president would be interested."

I winced inside, thinking of the Great White Father.

Pastor Huber interrupted, turning to me. "Do you really want to teach these savages? You think they can learn?"

I clenched my teeth, controlling my anger. "Yes," I said quietly. "They can learn."

"We can attempt it for three months," Pastor Aken continued, "and then reevaluate."

"Only an experiment," Pastor Huber said. "For three months." He fixed his gaze on me.

Then he turned to Pastor Aken. "We will need to send the reservation interpreter to see if the elders are willing to attempt this. They have not been easy to work with."

Slowly, I began to realize that I was going to be allowed to return to my people as their teacher.

"It is only an experiment, Sarah. You understand this?" Pinch Finger said.

"Yes," I said, resisting the urge to scream in joy. "Yes."

✻ ✻ ✻

The other girls crowded around me that night.

"Why were you called away from lessons?" Walks Tall asked.

"Who were those men? Why were they here?" Moon Awake demanded.

"Four Winds, what is happening?" Walks Tall touched my arm.

"I want to teach. I need to leave," I said, feeling the threat of tears. Leaving these girls, my sisters, would be more difficult than I thought.

"Why?" Laughing Deer asked, her lip trembling.

"To be a bridge," I answered.

TWENTY-SIX
RUNS WITH COURAGE

It seemed both strange and fitting that I would be carried back to my tiospaye the same way I had first left, in the white man's wagon.

I gathered my little rabbit, my wotawe, my shawl, and my slate board into a small satchel. I said good-bye to Walks Tall and Moon Awake. The three of us were determined to be brave, but each of us had cried as we embraced. Then I had gone to find Catches Fire.

"Join me," I said, when I found him outside the schoolhouse. "My tiospaye will accept you as one of us."

He looked down.

"My place is here," he said quietly, studying the ground.

"Please?" I begged. "You are my brother."

"William!" someone called, and I looked over to see the other girls beckoning for him to join them in their game.

They admired him, considered him a friend. They needed him.

"My place is here," he said, and I understood.

"It is the ultimate act of bravery to get close enough to touch an enemy in battle and not harm him," he said.

"Yes." I nodded.

"You have found your own way to count coup." He held out a small strip of leather toward me.

I felt a lump rising in my throat. I swallowed hard, trying not to cry. I took the leather strap and noticed it had several tally marks on it.

"This will be a reminder to you," he said. "It will help you remember all that you have learned here, both what you can see and what you cannot see."

I held his hands tightly before me, letting my tears fall.

Laughing Deer appeared. "Sarah, Sarah!"

"Be brave, little one," I said, leaning over and kissing her forehead.

Catches Fire took her hand and led her back toward the schoolhouse.

"The girls are playing a new game. It is so fun!" Laughing Deer babbled excitedly as she followed him.

I turned and walked to the white wagon.

✳ ✳ ✳

After a long winter's slumber, the prairie had awakened. Plants were starting to turn green and the grasses were already knee-high. Soon flowers would bloom and the entire prairie would erupt with color to celebrate winter's end.

My heart quickened to see the edges of jagged cliffs in the distance, knowing Makoce Sica and my tiospaye were close. I clutched the sides of the wagon as I watched the tipis grow larger. We were almost home.

Mother stood outside. Several aunts were next to her and Bear was nearby with some of the cousins. He had grown taller since I had last seen him.

I let out a shaky breath, not realizing I had been afraid to see them. I had been afraid they would look thin and unhealthy. But they looked well. My sacrifice had kept them safe. I gripped the wagon harder to keep myself from jumping out and running to them.

Pastor Huber and the interpreter stepped down from the cart and were brought into the council lodge with several elders. I smiled as they met, knowing how frightening the lodge would seem to the pastor.

☼ ☼ ☼

My entire tiospaye ate together that night beneath the stars. The elders traded stories back and forth, and I closed my eyes, letting the sound of their voices fill me with something I had been missing for so long.

Someone began a drumbeat, and several of the cousins danced. I joined, not caring that I was clumsy and that I could never dance as well as Cousin. Energy surged through me, and I danced for what I had left behind and for what I had reclaimed. I danced because I knew I would never have to hide my dance again.

After everyone had quieted I sat around the fire with Uncle and Mother and Father. It was a clear night, and the moon was bright and full.

"Before, you ran away from there to here. You ran away from something," Uncle said.

"Yes, Uncle."

"And now you have run from there to here. You have run to something."

I nodded.

"As I said before, sometimes you have to stay and sometimes you have to run. It takes courage to know the difference."

"It does," I said.

"Both of your runnings took great courage. Because of this, we will now call you Runs With Courage."

I shivered to hear this new name. It was a strong, brave name. I was proud to have earned it.

"Runs With Courage," Father repeated, and Mother nodded.

"Yes," I said, letting the name settle into my thoughts.

✳ ✳ ✳

In the warm days to follow, I found myself walking along the edge of Makoce Sica. Ignoring my fear of high places, I climbed to the topmost cliff and looked down at the small valley of stone below. Its colors were always most vibrant during this season. Lines of red and yellow danced across the rock. If I squinted, I could imagine Cousin running through the valley with her long graceful legs. In my memory I could travel back to a time when we would explore together and laugh and dream.

I knew things would never be the same. It was a new world, a white world, as Uncle had said. I knew that we would never leave the reservation and return to our beautiful He Sapa, just as I would never hear the sound of Cousin's laugh again.

But I would be like the wind. I would run strong and free and fast. I would carry the knowledge and understanding I now had. I would run with courage to bring my people what they would need.

EPILOGUE

The wind blew coldly outside our tipi. For a moment I stopped, hoping if I listened carefully enough, I would be able to hear the ancestors speak through the winds. But as always, in our home on the prairie, I could not.

The season was in change. Even though it was still cold, the air outside had already begun to grow warmer. Soon I would be able to hear the sound of crickets singing their lullaby at night. I looked forward to the time when the prairie would awaken from its winter slumber and burst into bloom. There was always hope in the changing of the seasons.

Bear stepped in through the tipi flap, and I smiled. He was in his own time of change. He was nearly as tall as I was. I knew it would not be long before he would be taller. At almost ten seasons, he was well on his way to becoming a man.

He was eager and quick and I was proud of all that he had learned in the past seasons of my teaching. He was almost equal with my own knowledge and had even started teaching some of the younger cousins. They treated the English words as if they were a fun game. But he knew the seriousness of the learning. The student was fast becoming the teacher.

"Let us work on letter writing," I said.

Bear nodded. Together we had learned that there were two kinds of letters in the white world: those that formed words and those that the whites used to communicate with each other. The practice of letter writing was an important way of communicating for the whites, and we both wanted to better learn how to do this. It felt strange to speak to someone who was not next to you. We had been practicing by writing pretend letters to each other.

Bear leaned over his slate and began writing.

I looked down at my slate, unsure of how to begin my own practice letter. Absently, I fingered the leather strap I carried with me always and had a sudden longing to write a letter to Catches Fire.

The meetings I now had every year with school officials took place in town buildings, far away from the school. I had not been allowed to visit the school or see either teachers or students. When I asked about Catches Fire, I was ignored. Eventually, I stopped asking.

I did not often allow myself to think of him or of my days at the school. It caused too much pain in my heart. But now I let my mind slip away from our tipi, away from our tiospaye, and on to the school. Was Catches Fire still at the school? Was he keeping well? And Laughing Deer. She would be much older now. What of her?

I pictured the faces of Walks Tall and Moon Awake and felt tears fall down my face.

"Sister, what are you thinking?"

Bear's voice startled me, and I looked over to see him watching me.

"You cry," he said.

"Yes," I answered.

"What are you thinking?" he repeated, and placed his hands in his lap, waiting for me to say more. Despite my tears, I smiled. He was becoming more like Uncle in the way he would stop and listen carefully.

"It has been so many seasons since I left the school," I said.

"Years, according to the white man's calendar. And yet their faces still fill my mind. I wish to know of Laughing Deer. And Catches Fire. Are they well?"

"Perhaps you should write them a letter," he said.

In this way he was still my little brother—naïve and optimistic in what he wanted. I knew the school officials would never allow Catches Fire to receive a letter.

"I wouldn't know where to send it. I don't think it would ever reach him," I said.

"I will write a letter to Catches Fire," Brother said matter-of-factly, erasing his practice letter on his slate and starting a new one.

I looked down at my own slate and pictured Catches Fire. His face was forever frozen clearly in my mind, even though I knew time would have changed how he looked.

Instead of a letter, I began to write about the first time I had seen Catches Fire, when he had burned my clothes.

I wrote without stopping, without really thinking, just letting the words pour out of me. As I wrote, I realized I wanted to write down all that had happened at the school. I wanted to write everything about Catches Fire and Laughing Deer, using white words so the whites could read their stories. When I ran out of space on my slate, I searched through my teaching supplies, finding some of the few pieces of paper I had. Carefully, I also pulled out the small bottle of ink and my ink pen.

I would write words that were permanent and could not be erased. I would write for those who had not been allowed to speak, and I would tell their stories.

I filled the pen with ink and I began.

AUTHOR'S NOTE

To the Lakota people of the Oceti Sakowin Native American tribe, He Sapa (Black Hills) is sacred ground, the place of their creation. For thousands of years the Lakota people lived in or near He Sapa, traveling to different camps according to the seasons. They believed all living things were sacred, and sustained themselves primarily with buffalo, using every part of the animal for food, clothing, tools, and toys.

In the 1800s white settlers began traveling and settling across the Dakota plains. The discovery of gold in various places as well as government policy brought this expansion and with it came conflicts between settlers and Native Americans, as well as between Native American tribes themselves. In an attempt to bring peace to the region, the United States government signed a number of treaties with different Native American groups.

Most applicable to the characters in this story was the Fort Laramie Treaty of 1868. This treaty stated that the Lakota agreed to settle within the Black Hills reservation of the Dakota Territory. They would not leave the confines of the Black Hills, and settlers would not be allowed in this area.

For a short while, the government upheld this treaty. Then, on a scouting expedition in 1874, General George Custer discovered gold near present-day Deadwood in the Black Hills. Waves of miners flooded in, seeking riches. Initially the government made vague attempts to uphold the 1868 treaty and kept settlers away. But in December of 1875, the commissioner of Indian Affairs ordered that all Sioux bands must move to reservations located on the prairies of present-day South Dakota. By this point the Indian Appropriations Act had declared that the U.S. government would no longer negotiate treaties with Native Americans.

To this day the Lakota people are fighting to reclaim their right to the Black Hills.

One tragedy of this time period (and the focus of this story) was the practice of putting Native American children into white-run boarding schools.

Such boarding schools began appearing in the 1880s. Some were funded by the federal government, but many were sponsored and run by Christian churches. Eventually, there were dozens of Indian boarding schools located throughout the United States.

The Carlisle Indian Industrial School in Pennsylvania, established in 1879, was one of the first of such schools. It was overseen by Colonel Richard Pratt, the person who coined the phrase "Kill the Indian in him, and save the Man." As this phrase became popular, it was shortened simply to "Kill the Indian, save the man."

The Carlisle School became a model for many of the boarding schools. It was run on the philosophy that the "Indian" in Native American children needed to be erased and replaced by white beliefs, culture, and religion. To do this, the school was managed with strict discipline and adherence to rules.

Some Indian parents sent their children to boarding schools willingly, believing it would help them navigate the white culture. Most parents did not, and their children were taken by threat or by violence.

The children at these schools were thrust into a world where everything was completely new to them: the food, the dress, the customs, and the traditions. They were taken away from the only support system they had ever known and thrown into a lonely and isolated existence. Children were punished for speaking in their native language and for continuing to participate in important cultural practices, such as dancing. They were not allowed to wear their own clothing, and their hair was cut, which violated one of their most basic belief systems.

Abuse in the schools was rampant. Many children ran away. Some died from illness and others languished from loneliness and neglect.

By the mid-1900s most of the schools had closed, although a few are still in existence today. Although the Carlisle Indian Industrial School no longer exists, the 186 graves of Indian children who died while attending this school remain in a graveyard near the original site of the school.

※ ※ ※

As a child I lived in the Black Hills of South Dakota. I grew up hiking and exploring the woods, surrounded by the scent of pine. It is a place of incredible beauty, with a feeling of peace that cannot be found elsewhere.

Although I knew some of the history of the Black Hills, it wasn't until I was researching the gold rush of Deadwood as an adult that I learned the settlement itself was illegal, a direct violation of the 1868 Fort Laramie treaty. This discovery led to more research, which eventually led to the Native American boarding schools—and this story.

The experience of children in these boarding schools holds difficult truths about our country's history. It is an important story, one that I felt compelled to tell. My hope is that I have given some voice to the children whose voices were lost so long ago.

JOAN M. WOLF

Joan M. Wolf is both a writer and a teacher. She is the author of the middle-grade novel *Someone Named Eva* (Clarion Books) as well as several teacher resource books. She has taught all ages, from children to adult, and is currently an elementary school teacher. She lives in Minnesota, where she attempts to stay warm during the winter months. Learn more about Joan at joanmwolf.com.